# Samurai High

To Debi,

# Samurai High

*A Novel*

*Jonathan Forrest*

iUniverse, Inc.
New York Bloomington Shanghai

**Samurai High**



iUniverse books may be ordered through booksellers or by contacting:

iUniverse
1663 Liberty Drive
Bloomington, IN 47403
www.iuniverse.com
1-800-Authors (1-800-288-4677)



ISBN: 978-0-595-47897-2 (pbk)
ISBN: 978-0-595-60097-7 (ebk)

Printed in the United States of America

For my mother Dorri
and
my grandmother Laura.
The two most wonderful women
I have ever known.

# 1

*They dragged the boy into the chamber; the tops of his bare feet sliding across the floor. His head sagged, and his fair hair hung down like a wet, dirty mop. They threw his slight body at the foot of the stairs and he fell to his hands and knees.*

*"What is your name?" asked a loud and booming voice from high above. It was the voice of the judge.*

*The boy remained silent.*

*"What is his name?"*

*"He has not yet given name, my Lord."*

*"How old are you?" asked the judge.*

*The boy did not respond.*

*"How old is the criminal?" the judge asked again.*

*"The boy is believed to be of his fourteenth year, my Lord," the guard replied.*

*"So young … so sad," the judge said. "Get him to his feet for sentencing."*

*The guard nodded and lifted the boy to stand, holding him there with a tight grip.*

*"Can he stand on his own?" the judge asked.*

*"He can."*

*"Then let him."*

*The guard stepped away, leaving the boy to stand on his own.*

*"Do you know why you are here?" asked the judge.*

*The boy was silent.*

*"Is the boy without voice?"*

*"No he is not, my Lord."*

*"Then why does he not speak?"*

*"Because he is ashamed, my Lord."*

*"Is this true boy? Do you not speak because you are ashamed of the crimes you have committed?"*

*The boy remained silent.*

*"I will assume this is the reason," the judge said. "As I will assume that you regret these crimes that you have committed. As I will assume that the gods will forgive you, even as you suffer in the depths of hell."*

*The judge turned to another man in the chamber, who wore a long dark cloak and held a glowing orb.*

*"What are his fears?" the judge asked the man.*

*"Death, dark, and spiders," the man replied, staring deep into the orb.*

*"Then we shall give him all three, shall we not?"*

*"Yes, my Lord."*

*"Boy," said the judge, "ronin boy, you have been tried and convicted of horrendous, unspeakable crimes against humanity, and you will pay for these crimes. Yes you will. You are hereby sentenced to be stripped of all your memories, except for your fears, and banished to the wells. But before you are taken to the dungeons, I ask you, do you have anything to say on your behalf?"*

*Slowly the boy raised his head, and for the first time faced the judge who sat high above. The boy's hair hung in his eyes like wet kelp, and his eyes rolled, like a shark, to the man holding the orb. He glared.*

*"Let me commit seppuku," said the boy in a low, defeated, voice. "Please."*

*"Never" the judge replied. "You shall die in the wells with the rest of the honorless filth. This is my final decision. You deserve no better. Take him away."*

*The guards came forward and pulled the boy from the chamber. They dragged him down to the dungeons, but did not return him to his cell. Instead, they took him to the end of the long hallway and through the last door. Inside this last room was a single well, its round stone surface about as high as a man's waist.*

*They brought the boy to the well, striped him of all his clothes, and without pause or ceremony, threw him in head-first. The boy splashed down into cold water and sank, but then began to kick and rise, breaking the surface with a gasp and a cry.*

*It was as dark as night. He could not see anything, not even his hands.*

*The boy began to tremble as he groped about and felt the wet, slippery sides of the well. He kicked his feet and floated in place, and soon he could hear the distant sound of a door opening above. A lantern was placed over the well and it blinded him. He shielded his eyes.*

*"May the gods have mercy on your soul," said a voice from above.*

*Then the figure dropped a small glowing object into the well and it landed beside him with a splash. At once, the well's darkness transformed into a bright whiteness, and the boy held his head and wailed.*

*"Stop!" he screamed.*

*A few moments passed, and the glowing orb rose from the well, up into the hands of the man waiting above as though he had reeled it up with an invisible string. The man stared into the orb and smiled.*

*"Goodbye, ronin boy," he said, and disappeared from view.*

*A moment later, two figures appeared in his place and immediately emptied two buckets into the well. The contents came tumbling down atop him: strange, dark shapes, like falling silhouettes, splashing the water about.*

*Glop. Glop. Glop.*

*Then something landed on his head with a dull thud. He reached up and felt a hairy, moving spider, scurrying down onto his face. The boy screamed and recoiled, as another landed on him.*

*The guards above called for more buckets of spiders and promptly emptied them into the well. Once their buckets were emptied, they called for more. And then more.*

*The boy sunk below the water, frantically trying to shake free all the spiders crawling on him. But as soon as he resurfaced, the spiders clung to him, all over his hair and face.*

*Finally, the lantern went dark and the door slammed shut. Now there was nothing but silent darkness.*

*The boy screamed again, but was interrupted by a hairy spider slipping into his mouth.*

# 2

Jaden woke with a gasp and a cry, and sat up in his bed. He was twisted about in the sheets and blankets and pillows as though he had been wrestling with them. He was hot and sweaty, even though the fan was blowing directly upon him. He reached over and turned off the fan and let his hand hang there on the knob for a while. It was a big old box fan that was once new and white, but was now layered with black dust on the inside edges.

His eyes fluttered and he was almost back to sleep when the alarm went off—a startling *beep, beep, beep*. He pounded his fist on the alarm to silence it, and slowly drifted back to sleep. But then it sounded again—*beep, beep, beep*—which brought another silencing jolt from his fist. This continued for another half-hour.

# 3

*The surface of the water had become alive—a living, breathing blanket of twitching life. Every time the boy broke the water's surface for air, this blanket of life would greet him with converging desperation. The boy had been underwater for a long time now, but didn't want to go back up for air; it was madness to do so. But he must. His lungs ached and throbbed and forced him up, up, up.*

*He felt the weight of the living blanket, like hands forcing him down, as he broke the surface, and he had to kick extra hard to get through it to the air.*

*He gasped and breathed as what seemed like hundreds of spiders clung to him, holding on even after he went back under. He twisted and thrashed and pulled them off, but some had become tangled in his hair. He could feel them as they felt him with their many legs, and he slapped and punched at himself, hoping to squash them to death. But there were always more, and they were always clinging.*

*He dove deeper, trying to distance himself from the frightening, disgusting blanket above. He swam and swam, and eventually touched bottom. He anchored himself there, arms and legs outstretched, so that he might stay.*

*For what? Forever? Already, his chest was burning again, begging him to go back up for air. But to what end? For how long would he continue? For how long could he?*

*Air bubbles left him in a rush and he shook his head, trying to force away the pain inside him. But it would not go. It only grew, and grew.*

*The boy kicked out against the well in a fury and was about to go back up when he felt the well give way. He stopped and spun around, and began to grope through the watery darkness, temporarily forgetting his need for air. He ran his hands over the walls of the well, searching for the spot his foot had struck. He found it; the stone had slid in a bit. He again pushed against this spot, but nothing moved. The stone had slightly given way, but that was as far as it was going to go. Suddenly, the pain in his chest returned.*

*For a moment, he stayed where he was at the very bottom of the well, with his fists clenched, his toes curled, and his face scrunched. He opened his mouth and screamed the last of his air and lashed out at the walls with kicks and punches. The pain was nothing compared to his need for air.*

*Perhaps the spiders were nothing, too. He would have to go up again. He must.*

*But he didn't.*

*At the last possible moment, the stone he had kicked and punched so violently suddenly gave way, and the boy felt the pull of the water rushing into the unseen hole. He felt around and realized that the hole might be just big enough to slip through and without much thought on the possible consequences the boy steeled himself and squeezed through the opening.*

# 4

Jaden showered with hot water and soap—lots of lather—and when he stepped from the shower his skin was red, like a lobster's. He toweled off and wiped the fog from the mirror, or at least attempted to. He stared at the face across from him, at the eyes.

Time passed.

When he finally left the bathroom, the steam rolled out behind him like a hot, humid breath.

# 5

*The surface of the pond was without blemish or ripple. It was as smooth as a mirror, and the predawn light highlighted it with a wink of reflection. The boy broke the surface of the water, shattering the mirror-like surface. He gasped for air, his mouth open to the sky, and breathed and breathed in air and life. He slowly began calming down and began to take in his surroundings.*

*He was floating in the middle of a small pond that was sheltered by thick, lush trees. He began to swim.*

*When he reached the shore, his feet touched the bottom of the pond. He walked out of the water and instantly remembered he was naked. He stood on the banks of the pond for a few moments, and then began to make his way through the trees.*

*It was a forest. The ground was covered in thick moss and pinecones. As he walked, he occasionally stepped on a stone or acorn. It hurt, but not much, and he walked until he reached a clearing and saw a small cabin with a slight twirl of smoke rising from its chimney. He watched and listened, but heard nothing, so he came closer. He spotted some clothes hanging on a line, and helped himself to a few.*

*He quickly dressed, putting on a pair of black hakima pants—a bit too baggy for his taste, but pants nonetheless—and a matching black top, which was also a tad loose. He saw a pair of sandals on the stoop by the back door and quietly snatched them up. They fit perfectly, even comfortably. Once he was fully dressed, he leaned in close to the door and listened.*

*As he bumped it slightly, the door creaked ajar. He stepped back for a moment and waited—nothing. He pushed the door open with the tip of his foot and stepped inside to a small kitchen. He could smell things—good things—and saw pots stewing on the stove, with steam rising from a kettle by the fireplace. The boy went to the stove, snatched up a long wooden spoon, and sampled what was cooking in the pot. It was very good, so he sampled from another, then another. He noticed a pie cooling on the windowsill. He stuck his finger in it. It was warm—blueberry, and near perfect. He used the same spoon to scoop up a piece, hardly bothering to chew it before swallowing.*

*Suddenly, he heard whistling coming from outside. He froze, the spoon still halfway in his mouth, as the whistling drew closer. He lowered the spoon and looked around frantically, trying to figure out what to do. He rushed to another doorway, trying to remain silent, and found himself standing in a wide living room. It was plain and simple, with a couch and chair, and a table with a lantern and an open book sitting on it. The boy searched frantically for a place to hide, but could not find one.*

*Finally, he spotted a trunk in the corner of the room. It was a fair-sized trunk, perhaps big enough to squeeze into. He unlatched it and flipped it open, and saw the katana.*

*It was a beautiful weapon, encased in a polished black sheath. For a moment, the boy stared at it, hypnotized. But the sound of the back door opening and footsteps snapped him back to reality. He climbed into the trunk with the katana and carefully lowered the top just as he heard the whistling abruptly stop.*

*"Is somebody here?" called out a man's voice. "If there is someone still in this home, you must know that you are trespassing."*

*The footsteps drew closer, crossing the kitchen. The boy hunkered low on his side, curled tight, and squeezed the katana in his hands, as though it would make things right and keep him hidden and safe.*

*The footsteps paused, then came closer, much closer. Then silence.*

*"Come out of the trunk, please. I know you're in there."*

*The boy scrunched his face and took a deep breath. He hesitated, then opened the trunk and sat up. He froze, unable to move, overwhelmed with confusion.*

*There was no man at all—and no room. He looked down and saw that he was no longer sitting in the same trunk; the one that now surrounded him was older, beaten, and broken, and filled with dirt and weeds.*

*He got to his feet and saw he was standing in the middle of an open field.*

# 6

His room was messy. As he began to get dressed, Jaden had to search for his clothing—a sock beneath a pillow, one sneaker behind the hamper, the other inside the hamper, a tee shirt on top of the small television, a pair of pants draped over the head board, and a fresh, clean pair of underwear peeking out of the top dresser drawer. He dressed quickly and stood before the tall mirror on his bedroom door, looking again at the boy who stared back at him.

The boy was young, slim, and of average height. His pants were baggy—"raver wear," with a drawstring that hung down past his knees. His tee shirt was white and plain. The boy's hair was a blond mop that cascaded down, framing his face like golden wings.

He stared at himself for a while, his mouth twisted and unsure. Finally, he opened the door and went downstairs.

He walked into the kitchen and plopped down at the table, slumping. His mother had her back to him, cooking eggs on the stove. Her hips swiveled to the holiday music coming from the small radio on the countertop.

"Kath, can you turn that down a bit?" his father demanded from behind the newspaper he held high that it hid his face. "Not even—"

The rest of his complaint went unheard as he shook the paper to satisfaction.

His mother muttered something, then turned down the volume. She began to hum, as if to compensate for the lack of noise.

Seated to his right in a high-chair was his baby brother Tommy. He wore a diaper and a baby-blue bib that was already stained with what looked like equal parts apple sauce and oatmeal. Tommy reached forward in his seat, extending his arms outward to reach the rattle that rested on the table top just beyond his reach. Jaden slid the rattle into his brother's hands and then slouched back in his seat.

Tommy took the rattle and began to shake it. He threw Jaden a toothless smile. Jaden grinned back.

Without even slightly lowering his newspaper, his father reached over and snatched the rattle away from Tommy and placed it farther away, toward the center of the table.

For a moment, Tommy did nothing, confused by the sudden turn of events. Then his mouth sagged open, his lips quivered, and his eyes began to shimmer as he started to cry.

"Kath," his father said, almost pleading.

Without a word, his mother reached back and placed a pacifier in Tommy's mouth. Then she was instantly back at the stove.

Tommy began to suck.

Jaden turned his attention to the only other person sitting at the table: his grandfather. He sat quietly, his body slumped almost depressingly in his seat. His hair was grey, wiry, and balding, and his face was a road map of wrinkles. His left eye was dead with cataracts and drooped like a runny egg. His nostrils were encrusted with snot. His upper-lip and chin were spotted with whiskers, and a pool of drool formed at the corner of his mouth, threatening to drip away. His whole body shook and shuddered as though he were in the throes of a never-ending chill. He faced Jaden vacantly, emptily, and without a word.

Jaden's mother turned around, pan in hand, and began serving breakfast. First to his father, scooping a healthy portion of scrambled eggs onto his plate. Then his grandfather. Then Jaden.

The toast popped and at the same moment the phone rang. His mother answered the phone and simultaneously began to butter the toast.

"Oh hello, Jill," his mother said. "Yes … oh yes, I remembered."

She turned to Jaden and mouthed, "Your grandfather. Please."

Jaden sighed and slid his chair closer to his grandfather. He took his spoon, scooped up a small portion of eggs, and brought the spoon up to his grandfather's mouth. For a moment his grandfather did nothing. Then his lips began to quiver and part. He fed him a mouthful and watched him carefully to make sure he chewed and then swallowed. When he had successfully finished the first bite, Jaden scooped up another spoonful and repeated the process.

"Dad," Jaden began softly, somewhat hesitantly.

His father either didn't hear him or simply ignored him.

"Dad," he said again, this time a little louder.

His father sighed, ruffled the paper between them, and said "What?" with clear annoyance.

"Um … I was … I mean I wanted to tell you some—" Jaden stammered.

"Kath," his father said abruptly cutting him off, "where's my goddamned coffee already?"

His mother wrapped up her conversation and quickly hung up the phone. She began to pour his coffee.

"Dad," Jaden tried again.

"Jaden!" his mother snapped.

He noticed that his grandfather had managed to spit his eggs back down his chin and onto his shirt.

His father, for the first time since Jaden had entered the kitchen, lowered an edge of the paper as Jaden's mother began to clean his grandfather. His father eyed Jaden for a beat.

"Watch what you're doing, huh?" his father said before again lifting the newspaper.

When his mother was done cleaning his grandfather, she said to Jaden, "Keep an eye on him, okay?"

It was not said unkindly or as a reprimand, like his father, but rather as a cautionary reminder from a very busy woman. His mother turned and was back to tending his father's coffee.

"Mom?" Jaden said.

"Yes honey?"

"I—"

Tommy spit out his pacifier and began to fuss.

His father sighed loudly. "Will somebody do something about that?" he snapped.

"Jaden, honey, could you?" his mother said. "My hands are full."

Jaden placed the pacifier back into his brother's mouth, but Tommy just spit it out again and continued to fuss. Jaden tried the pacifier again and was met with the same result.

"I think he's hungry or something," Jaden said.

"No, no," his mother said. "He's already been fed. He probably just wants to be held, that's all."

Without a word, Jaden stood and pulled his brother from the highchair and held him. He playfully whispered something to his brother, which stopped Tommy's crying. Tommy took hold of Jaden's long hair and began to play with it, and chew it. Jaden let him.

His mother placed the cup of coffee in front of his father and added a couple pieces of toast to his plate. She opened the refrigerator and began rummaging about. His father silently reached for the cup, took a sip, and lowered it back to the table top. He turned a page.

A long, silent moment passed.

"Mom, Dad," Jaden said, rocking Tommy softly.

Neither responded.

"I've been wanting to talk to you both, and I—"

"Faggots," his father blurted, clearly responding to something he had just read in the paper. "Trying to get married … should pack 'em up and ship 'em off to some god-forsaken island somewhere. Let 'em live their little homo lives elsewhere."

He turned the page.

Jaden stopped rocking his brother. He stood still.

"What were you saying honey?" his mother said coming up from the refrigerator with a new stick of butter in her hand.

"Nothing," Jaden said softly.

Tommy began to cry.

# 7

*Finally the boy got out of the trunk and scanned the vast emptiness around him. In every direction was a sea of green knee-high grass blowing in a soft warm breeze. The boy closed his eyes tight, counted to ten, and then reopened them. The field remained. Gone was the cabin with the kitchen of foods, and the forest and pond were nowhere to be found, either.*

*Maybe his mind was gone, too.*

*He felt his chest pounding; a thousand questions swirled through his young mind, and he struggled to find an answer for even a single one. He suddenly felt dizzy and ill, and he sat down in the swirling grass and rested for a while. When he finally stood, he returned to the trunk and saw to his surprise that the black sheathed katana was still resting there at the bottom. The boy eyed the katana for a moment, wondering if it, too, would suddenly disappear.*

*It did not.*

*He slowly reached down and took it. Still it did not disappear; it was real. He gripped it tightly, as though doing so might prevent it from vanishing.*

*He took a deep, steeling breath and slung the katana over his shoulder, where it hung by a simple rope loop. Staring off into the distance, he nodded to himself and began to walk. The grass blew softly at his legs, and his hair was tossed in the breeze. He walked and walked, until finally, the field gave way to a simple dirt road. He stopped and looked left, then right. Both ways looked the same, and stretched on forever, so he chose to turn left—and walked on.*

*Wild weeds grew on the dirt road and were thick in some places, almost hiding the road altogether in some spots. Eventually, the road took on wagon trails, and he quickened his pace. The road wound up a slight hill. When he reached the top, he saw a farmhouse, a kite flying high in the air behind it.*

*As he ran down the hill toward the farmhouse, he saw the kite lowering. Before he could reach the bottom of the hill, the kite disappeared from sight. He ran down the dirt road and reached the farmhouse, breathing hard. He circled around to its back, where the kite-flyer would have been. But all he found was a kite tangled around a tree, drifting just above the ground. Then a strong wind came through and again lifted the kite high into the air. With a sigh, the boy turned back to the house.*

*The farmhouse looked old, with faded, sun-baked, red paint peeling from its sides. A back screen door hung crooked on one hinge and the windows on the first floor were broken out. The house appeared abandoned. Undaunted, the boy cautiously approached the house, pulled aside the screen door, and tried the knob. It was unlocked, and he pushed the door open with a loud, whiny creak.*

*"Hello? Is anybody here?" he called out.*

*There was no answer, so he stepped inside. The air was thick, almost unbreathable, and carried a strange smell—faint, but foul. He rubbed his nose.*

*Suddenly, he heard the sound: a banging, scuffling, and scurrying. Instinctively, he pulled his new katana from its sheath and held it out before him at the ready. It struck him that he had held one before.*

*"Hello?" he called out again.*

*No answer.*

*"Is there somebody here? I do not mean to trespass. I only have a question or two."*

*There came another sound, this time closer; a rattling from a room out of sight. The boy stood still, waiting and listening. Suddenly, there came a growl, and a dark creature shot from the shadows and raced toward him. He managed to dive out of the way at the last moment as the creature lunged for him and sailed past through the open doorway. The boy jumped to his feet and looked just in time to see the dog spinning around and charging back toward him, its teeth bared and growling savagely. The boy slammed the door just as the dog jumped again; the smash against the door rattled its frame. The dog began to bark angrily, clawing at the door. Then it faded away, as if it were racing around the side of the house.*

*The boy looked around, not moving a muscle. Suddenly, he heard the dog coming in through the front of the house. The boy bounded up the stairs directly in front of him, taking them two or three at a time. Just as he reached the top stair, he saw the dog round the corner into the entryway below. The dog saw him and barked viciously, and raced up the stairs. The boy turned and ran along a hallway. Coming to a door at its end, he pulled the door open and slipped inside. He locked the latch just as the dog reached the door, ramming and clawing at it.*

*The boy stepped back from the door, not noticing where he stepped. He bumped into something and instantly whirled around. He saw a figure of the person in the shadows, and reflexively attacked with his katana, swinging for the head. The next sound he heard was the mirror in which he's seen his own reflection shattering into thousands of tiny pieces.*

*Breathlessly, he stood and stared at the shattered glass at his feet, his katana still pointed out before him.*

*The dog went quiet at the sound of the breaking glass, and the boy turned back to the door. After a few minutes, he looked around. He was in a small bathroom; a sink, a toilet, a tub, and nothing more. After a moment, he slowly made his way back to the door. He put his head to the door and listened. Nothing.*

*Suddenly, the dog smashed against the door with such fury that the boy fell away to his backside as the dog barked and scratched anew at the door.*

*"Go away!" the boy shouted. "Just go! Leave me alone!"*

*But the dog wouldn't hear of it. It attacked the door again and again, relentlessly. And so the boy slid away to the tub and rested on the floor with his back against it. It was only seconds later that he caught the first hint of the rancid odor. He turned his head and peered into the tub. Inside was a half-devoured corpse resting at the bottom—bone and rotting flesh—curled into a fetal position as though it were trying to hide.*

*The boy scrambled to his feet, hurried over to the window, and tried to lift it, but it had been nailed shut from the inside. He used the hilt of his katana to break out the dirty glass. He peered outside and saw a wide roof a few feet below the windowsill, slanting down over the front of the house. He climbed out and dropped down at a crouch, nearly losing his balance in the process. But he managed to steady himself, then stood and looked around.*

*There was nothing around. No place to go. Nowhere to hide.*

*He walked to the edge of the roof and looked down. It was a fairly long drop to the ground, but he was certain he could make it if he lowered himself by his hands, feet-first.*

*But where would he go from there?*

*His thoughts were interrupted by the sound of the growling. The dog had somehow made its way out onto the roof. Out of the corner of his eye, the boy could see another open window nearby.*

*"Calm down boy … calm down …" he said.*

*The dog bared its teeth and began to bark. Drool fell from the edges of its mouth.*

*The boy lifted his katana, ready for the onslaught.*

*The dog charged forward, jumped, and howled as the katana pierced its abdomen. But the dog had landed on him, and he lost his balance and tumbled backward off the roof.*

# 8

Jaden sat on his grandfather's bed and played his guitar for a while, strumming randomly at the strings again and again with his eyes closed. Time passed slowly.

# 9

*The boy splashed into the murky water of the bog. He climbed to his feet, drenched from head to toe, and looked around in awe. His surroundings had again changed abruptly. It was so disorienting. So maddening. So … impossible.*

*It now looked to be dusk, and the bog was white with a low-hanging mist. He turned this way and that, scanning his surroundings. Eventually, he realized he was still holding his katana in his grip. He sheathed it and slung it back over his shoulder.*

*"What is the meaning of this?" he yelled to the sky. A flock of dark birds, perhaps bats, darted into the air and disappeared.*

*The boy shook his head and brushed the wet hair from his face.*

*Something moved behind him. He spun around and pulled out his katana, but the bog was suddenly very still, and very quiet. He took a step away from the sound, hearing only the water that sloshed at his knees.*

*"Child …" a voice said.*

*The boy turned again.*

*"Who's there?" he blurted.*

*There was no answer.*

*"I heard you," the boy said, even if only trying to convince himself.*

*"What purpose does a child have in the swamps?" the voice finally replied. It was a whisper of a woman's voice.*

*"I don't know why I'm here," he replied. "I don't know where 'here' even is. Can you tell me?"*

*"Only a fool walks the swamps alone," the voice said, ignoring his question. "But a child—a child has never entered. What is your name, boy?"*

*"I—I do not know …" he said, his voice trembling with revelation. "I do not know my name!"*

*"You do not know your own name?" the voice replied, almost chuckling. "How can this be? Are you disturbed?"*

*"No. I mean … I don't know what's happening to me. I think I'm lost. I think—"*

*"Are you plagued?"*

*"No."*

*"I did not think so," the voice said. "I did not smell it on you."*

*The voice had changed from a whisper to a tone of lust, or desire. And now there was the sound of water parting and sloshing, and coming closer.*

*"Why are you here?" asked the boy, his voice guarded and nervous. He spun around as he heard the sound nearing.*

*"I am here because this is the only place I can be," the voice replied. "I cannot live beyond the swamp. I am not like you and the people who chased me here. I am … different."*

*The sloshing was coming ever closer. The boy held his katana out before him.*

*"How do I get out of here?" he asked.*

*"Why do you want to leave? You just arrived. Perhaps you would like to join me for a meal. I have not had a guest in a long, long time. We could dine together."*

*The sloshing was now loud, and very close.*

*"Stay away from me," he pleaded. "Please!"*

*"Why do you say this? Are you afraid of what you can't see?"*

*A slosh came so close that the boy felt the water ripple against his legs. He spun around.*

*"I said stay away!"*

*"Now you are being rude, child …" the voice said, now longing. "Ohh, child … I am sooo hungry."*

*The boy stood ready, his hands shaking as he gripped his katana. The bog was suddenly very quiet again.*

*Suddenly, the woman erupted from the water directly behind him. He turned just in time to see her pale, scaly face and long, dark hair. Her eyes were white and sickly. She was tall—taller by a body's length, and towered above him. Her arms were long and thin, and her hands were all fingers, lengthy and white.*

*"Come here!" she said, reaching for him.*

*He sliced out with his katana and severed her hands at the wrists. The bog woman wailed and dropped below the surface of the water. He turned and ran as fast as he could, splashing through the water. He could still hear the bog woman's wails as he tripped and fell headlong into the swamp.*

# 10

The door opened.

"Decided to come to school today?" Bill asked.

"Something like that," Jaden replied.

"Are you crazy? Just a hoodie? It's freezing outside ... like ten degrees."

"I know, Bill. Can I come in?"

"Oh, yeah."

Bill stepped aside, holding the door open, and then shut it once they were both inside. He was a taller boy, with dark hair and a widow's peak. He looked at Jaden, and at the guitar case he was carrying.

"Seventh period?"

Jaden nodded.

"I hate public speaking," Bill said with a sigh. "Why do we even have to take it anyway? Sucks."

"At least your speech is out of the way. It's better to get it done early, I think."

"Maybe. But you saw me. Nearly peed my pants."

"Yeah, your hands were shaking," Jaden said with a chuckle.

"I couldn't stop," Bill replied, shaking his head as he thought about the nightmare.

"You did all right. Better than Gloria."

Bill sighed and laughed.

"That's not saying much, is it?" he said.

"No, it's not."

Bill started to walk away.

"Wait in the living room," he said. "I still have to get ready."

"Hurry up."

"We got plenty of time."

"It's icy."

"We'll stop at the store and get some hot cocoa," Bill said as though this would solve everything.

Jaden could hear his friend running up the stairs to his bedroom. He walked into the living room and fell backward onto the couch, where he sat silently in the darkness.

# 11

*When he came back up from the water, gasping and groping, he found that the mist of the bog was gone. He took hold of something solid and pulled himself up. His eyes widened.*

*He was sitting in a bathtub half-full of warm, sudsy water. There was even a rubber duck floating at his feet.*

*The boy stared. He reached up and wiped the suds from his face, and sat for a moment pondering his new environment.*

*Suddenly, he heard the scream. Without thinking, he jumped from the tub and rushed to the closed bathroom door, his clothes dripping wet, and listened. He heard voices—muffled, angry, and afraid. He slowly turned the knob and inched the door open. He could see movement flash by, and he ducked back. But whatever had passed by the door did so without noticing him.*

*He again leaned forward and peeked through the crack. The room outside the door was darkened except for the dim light of a lamp. He could see a woman lying on the bed with her hands and feet tied behind her. Her mouth was gagged and she sobbed softly.*

*"Quiet!" came a male voice.*

*The boy saw the man come into view and grab the woman by the hair.*

*"You make one more sound and I'll slit your throat! You hear me bitch?"*

*The man pushed the woman's face into the mattress and stomped away to the other side of the room, out of sight. He could hear some commotion: things being broken, smashed, and thrown. A moment later, the man returned to the bed and leaned in close to his prisoner.*

*"Thirty bucks? Only thirty bucks?!" he said. "Where's the rest? Huh? Where?!"*

*The woman moaned and the man slapped the back of her head.*

*"Where's your jewelry? Huh?!"*

*The man again stomped away. Seconds later, the boy saw two dresser drawers fly through the air and crash into the far wall. The man cursed and was immediately back on the woman again. He flipped her over onto her back and pulled a knife from his side. The woman turned her head away and cried. The man straddled her and leaned in close, eyeing her, and then ripped her shirt open, revealing her breasts. He began to undo her pants. When the woman began to struggle, the man punched her in her face. She lay motionless and silent as he unzipped his pants.*

*The boy stepped from the bathroom and darted toward the bed. At the last second, the man turned.*

*"What the fu—"*

*His question was cut short by the sword ramming through his chest. For a moment, the man just stared at the boy, motionless, before blood began pouring from his mouth. He slumped from the bed to the floor and didn't move.*

*The boy stood there holding his now-bloody katana, his chest heaving. A faint sound quickly snapped him back to reality. He turned to see a little girl cowering in a dark corner of the room, watching him. She was naked and her eyes were wide with terror. As the boy took a step toward her, she buried her face in her arms and cried. The boy watched for another moment, then went to the bedroom door, opened it, and stepped out.*

# 12

The trash cans scraped on the icy ground as the boys dragged them down the walk and to the street. They left them by the curb and then climbed over a snow bank to reach the street and began to walk.

"Your mom's nice." Jaden said. "She offered to make me breakfast."

"She likes you." Bill said. "You're probably my only friend that she doesn't absolutely hate. She says you're sweet."

"I am sweet."

"Yeah, right."

"You know who *is* really sweet though …" Jaden began.

"Don't even say FanGloria."

"Gloria," Jaden corrected. "Well …"

"She's a beast."

"She likes you."

"Yeah I know … she only calls my house every day." He looked to Jaden with an accusing stare. "And I wonder how she got my number, anyway."

"You don't hate her that much."

"Well, whatever. But I certainly don't want to have sex with her."

"You know what they say …"

"What do they say?"

"Beggars can't be choosers."

"And you know what else they say?"

"What?"

"A pig wearing perfume is still a pig."

"Gloria's not a pig."

Bill shrugged. "You like her so much, why don't *you* have sex with her?"

Jaden paused. "Me and Gloria—"

"*Fan*Gloria." Bill interrupted.

"Me and *Gloria* … are like best friends. It's not close to like that. She doesn't even like me like that."

"Well, lucky you."

Jaden paused again. "Maybe if you just gave her a chance," he said.

"Did she put you up to this?" Bill asked.

Jaden looked away.

Bill let out a groan of disproval.

"Man, why can't you be friends with like Sara Pacouchy or something," he said. "I'd plow her like a winter storm."

Jaden laughed.

"Oh, and you wouldn't?" Bill said.

"I'm saving myself for marriage," Jaden replied.

They both laughed as Bill opened the door to the store. The bell above the door chimed as they entered.

"Hey," Bill said to the old clerk and waved.

"Hello, boys. Cold out there?" the clerk asked, obviously joking.

"Just a little," Bill said.

The boys walked over to the coffee and hot cocoa dispensers near the register.

"I don't have any money," Jaden said.

"On me," said Bill as he grabbed a Styrofoam cup.

They filled them and topped them and then placed their cups on the counter.

"Good thinking," the old clerk said. "You'll need it to survive out there today."

"Tell me about it."

"That will be three dollars even."

Bill handed over a ten-dollar bill, and as the old clerk reached for it he accidentally hit one of the cups and knocked it over. The cover popped off and it spilled over the countertop.

The boys stepped back.

"Jeez!"

"Woops!"

The old clerk frowned and came around the counter.

"Hold on," he said. "Let me get a few paper towels."

He began to stride off down an aisle toward the back of the store.

"Make yourself another," he said without turning.

The boys looked at each other.

"It was yours," Bill said.

"Actually, it was yours."

"Who's paying?" Bill asked, looking up at the ceiling.

Jaden grinned and stepped over to the dispenser. Bill folded back the top of his cocoa and took a sip. His eyes drifted to the shelf of magazines behind the counter—and the women on the covers.

Bill looked over his shoulder as the clerk disappeared into a back room. Then he looked to Jaden, who was just beginning to pour another drink.

"Pssst!" he said.

Jaden looked up, and Bill nodded to the back room.

"Keep an eye out."

Bill slipped around the counter, grabbed the closest magazine, zipped open his book bag, and stuffed it inside. He zipped it up and raced back around the corner just as the old clerk came back into view.

Jaden's mouth dropped open.

"Don't panic!" said the old clerk as he hurried back with what looked like a bunch of rolled-up toilet paper. "The cavalry has arrived!"

# 13

*As he stepped into a stairwell, the boy spun around and was shocked to see that the doorway he had just passed through was no longer there. In its place was a white metal door. It was filthy, and was decorated with colored words drawn all over it in different styles and patterns. He read some of the words and knew them to be curses, while others he didn't understand at all.*

*The boy grabbed hold of the metal handle and pulled; the handle came off in his hand. He tried pushing on the door, it but it wouldn't budge, and his attempts at reattaching the handle were futile. The boy eventually threw down the handle and cursed—it was, in fact, one of the very words written upon the door.*

*He turned and looked down the concrete stairwell. It was dark, though on some landings he could see single light bulbs encased in small cages of wire on the ceilings, and there was a foul smell of human waste. The boy frowned, took a deep breath, and started down the stairs. He reached the first half-landing, ten steps down, and saw another door one flight below. When he reached it, he tried the handle with a little more care. The handle did not fall off this time, but the result was the same: the door was locked.*

*He went down another set of stairs, found another door, and found it locked as well. Then he tried another flight and another locked door, then another, and another.*

*The boy kicked the door before him and winced at the pain that shot through his foot. Again he cursed. He stood there for a long moment as though trying to gather his thoughts and emotions.*

*Then the boy went down another flight and was surprised to see the doorless opening in front of him. He stepped down the last steps and looked out past the opening. He could see little. It seemed to be darker beyond the opening than it was in the stairwell. But it was the only way out; there was simply nowhere else to go.*

*As he stepped through, the first thing he noticed was the water at his feet; not as high as the swamp had been, but just as dark. Instinctively, he pulled out his katana and held it before him.*

*He paused and listened, but heard nothing, except for the sounds of dripping from afar. He remained motionless, deciding what to do.*

*Finally, he took another step forward. By now, his eyes had adjusted to the dim light, and he could see his surroundings more clearly. He seemed to be in an enclosed space that was wide and long. There was a fairly high ceiling, and he noticed some water dripping through cracks in the concrete above. Spread out before him were evenly placed pillars that reached from ground to ceiling in perfect rows that stretched for as far as he could see.*

*He began to walk, his feet in cool water up to his ankles, his every step echoing around him. He walked past the first set of pillars, moving slowly and cautiously, carefully listening. His eyes darted from one side to the other, scanning everything in front of him. So far, he had not encountered anything or anyone.*

*As he passed the second set of pillars, he spotted something up ahead. It was another doorway, lit brightly, and although it was quite far away, his pace quickened and his feet sloshed through the water.*

*As he neared the other doorway, he heard the distant sound of a door opening and slamming shut. He froze. The hairs on the back of his neck bristled and stood on end.*

*He turned and looked back. His eyes widened and his pulse quickened as he stared at the dark figure that was now standing in the opening of the stairwell from which he had just come.*

*For a long moment, the boy and the dark figure just faced each other, neither moving nor speaking. Only the sounds of water dripping and moving in the space between them could be heard.*

*Suddenly, the dark figure raced toward him. Although the sight of this unknown entity sprinting toward him terrified him, and even though he wanted nothing more than to be as far away from this spot as possible, the boy could not move. He was paralyzed with fear and it wasn't until the dark figure had reached the first series of pillars that he turned and ran for his life.*

*The boy ran and the dark figure followed, but the boy was running so hard and so fast, splashing water everywhere, that he could not hear what was chasing him. A quick glance over his shoulder made him realize that the dark figure was closing on him fast.*

*Suddenly, the boy tripped and fell, splashing down hard into the water. He scrambled to his feet quickly, stealing another look behind. The dark figure was closer now. The boy screamed out and raced on toward the lighted doorway ahead, which was now not far off.*

*He tripped again, but somehow managed to stay on his feet. He regained his full stride, grateful he had not fallen—doing so would have been the end of him for sure. But it didn't matter. All that mattered to him now was the doorway, which was getting closer.*

*Finally, he reached the door and jumped from the water into the doorway. He stood waiting, half-expecting to be whisked away from this present horror to another. But nothing happened. He was still there in the doorway.*

*As he turned to look back, he saw the dark figure was now very close, splashing through the water just past the last series of pillars. Now there was nothing between the boy and the dark figure except watery, open space.*

*The boy held his katana out in front of him. It was shaking hard in his trembling grip. Suddenly, he noticed that the doorway had a door—it was just wide open. He grabbed the door and swung the door shut with all his might, slamming it shut just as the dark figure lunged.*

*He stood where he was, shaking all over. The door was shut and the dark figure was on the other side of it. The boy backed up to the stairs, sat on the bottom step, and put his hands to his face, as if trying to hold his head together.*

*After what seemed to him like an eternity had passed, the door handle slowly creaked down. Terrified, the boy raised his head as the handle reached bottom and the door clicked unlocked. He jumped to his feet, his katana held high, as the door swung open. Before anyone or anything could move, he leapt forward lashing out with his blade and with a vicious battle cry …*

# 14

"Why's it so cold in here?"

"Heater's broken. Sorry," said the bus driver, a middle-aged woman named Peg, glancing in the rearview mirror.

"Can see my breath," Bill said rubbing his hands together. "Colder in here than outside."

Jaden nodded and hugged himself.

"They should at least give us blankets or something," Bill said.

"Well," Peg said, staring back at him in the view mirror, "come next week. The heat's still broken, I'll knit you one."

"Yeah, right."

"Yup," Peg said. "I'll even knit you matching mittens. That doesn't do ya, well, we could always just set up a campfire right there in the aisle. You could bring marshmallows."

Bill sighed. "You're so kind."

"That's what they tell me."

"Hey, Bill," Jaden said, "why don't you just wear those Bigfoot slippers your father's always wearing? They're styling."

Bill buried his face in his hands.

"Argh," he said. "My father is *so* retarded."

"He's cool," Jaden said. "Funny."

"Funny? Yeah if your idea of funny is wearing a tee shirt that says: What would Jesus do?"

Peg laughed.

"Well, he's still better than my dad." Jaden said.

"At least your dad isn't giving a sermon every second of every day."

"At least your dad talks to you at all."

"I'd prefer it if he didn't. Trust me."

"You think that," Jaden said.

"I *know* that. I'd give a million bucks if my dad would just shut up for one second and stop riding my ass."

Bill looked quick in the mirror and caught Peg's eye.

"Sorry," he said sheepishly. "I meant buttocks."

Peg laughed again, shook her head, and drove on.

# 15

*... and was stunned when his katana became lodged in a tree.*

*It was disorienting, and for a moment the boy stood still, waiting for his mind to catch up with his body. He looked around and saw that he was as far away from the underground space of pillars and water as he might possibly ever be.*

*He now found himself in a forest of thick trees and pine needles that covered the ground like a brown carpet.*

*He pulled his katana from the bark of the tree and took a deep breath. He stood on a sloping hillside, and the trees stretched on for as far as he could see.*

*"What is this?" the boy whispered to himself as a pine-scented breeze blew through and ruffled his clothing.*

*A flash of white caught the boy's eye. It passed below on the hillside between two trees, and then was gone. But as the boy stared, the same white shape came into view again, a little farther away. The boy's eyes narrowed, then widened, at what he saw.*

*It was a woman wearing a white dress.*

*"Hello?!" the boy called as he took a step in her direction. But the woman made no indication that she heard. She merely walked along and disappeared behind another tree.*

*The boy sheathed his katana and made his way down the hill toward her. When he was close enough, he called out to her again.*

*"Hello? Ma'am, may I ask you a few—"*

*But the woman wandered around another tree, her long white dress sweeping along the ground behind her, and disappeared from sight. The boy ran to catch up and as he came around the far side of the tree, he almost ran into her. She was carefully making her way down the hillside away from him. He stepped around her and into her path.*

*"Excuse me," he said.*

*But he stopped. The woman was carrying a long, silver screw-ended faucet in her hands, and wore a white blindfold that matched her dress and covered her eyes. She could not possibly see where she was going. And yet, she kept walking.*

*She stepped past him, as though he were just another tree in her path, and was on her way again without a word.*

*The boy watched her go for a moment, and then made his way to catch up again. He walked behind the woman and followed her as she made her way farther down the hillside. Eventually they came to more natural path and the woman turned onto it, as though she could see all that was before her through her blindfold. The boy followed.*

*She led him to a small clearing, where she finally stopped. The boy entered the clearing behind her, careful to keep a safe distance. He watched her, curious and unsure.*

*The woman walked to the far end of the small clearing and knelt before a large tree. She raised the faucet to just above her head and pushed it against the tree. Slowly, she began to turn the faucet, and after only a few rotations, the boy could see the screw end of the faucet was digging into the bark of the tree. She turned it one last time and the faucet was firmly attached to the side of the tree.*

*The boy stepped closer and watched as the woman positioned herself so her face was just beneath the faucet. She reached up and took hold the handle and began to turn. It made a tiny squeaking sound as though it needed oiling, and then the woman opened her mouth. For a long time, nothing happened. The woman in white just knelt there with her head raised, mouth open, and eyes blindfolded. Nothing. And then …*

*Something began to come out of the faucet. It was dark, and definitely not water. Perhaps a black liquid, a glob, slowly dripping, lowering—and wiggling.*

*The boy gasped and his own hand went to his mouth. He watched as the black thing lowered more. It was not a liquid at all, but a living creature; an insect, perhaps.*

*It had moving parts—legs—that wiggled in a hundred different directions, and as it dropped lower, the woman opened her mouth wider and wider. The squirming black creature touched her lips, its tiny legs flailing about as it descended into the woman's mouth. Now the black creature was coming down much faster than before. The boy watched with revulsion as the woman's throat began to bulge as the creature entered it.*

*And it came faster still, almost like a liquid, flowing straight down into the woman's mouth. She began to make gurgling, choking sounds, and her body started to sway as though it were rocking her from within. The boy began to gag at the sight before him, but could not pull his eyes away.*

*And then, suddenly, it was over. The last of the creature dropped from the faucet and into the woman's mouth, and was gone. The woman closed her mouth and lowered her head, and her body slumped forward as though she might have fallen asleep.*

*The boy became suddenly aware of how quiet the forest had fallen. He could hear only his own heavy breathing, and wasn't sure if he had been holding his breath this whole time.*

*The woman stirred, then stood. The boy took a step back away from her and heard himself swallow and swallow hard.*

*She turned to face him then, her hands at her sides her legs together, her face expressionless. Then she reached up and lowered the blindfold, revealing a sunken face and two empty sockets where her eyes should have been.*

*The boy jumped backward, letting out a whimper of shock and fear, his eyes wide and shimmering. Then he saw the black creature poke its way out of one eye socket and into the other, and he could actually hear its tiny legs wiggling along. Then the woman opened her mouth wide and lurched forward. The boy instinctively pulled out his katana as the woman reached for him, and instantly struck, severing her head from her body in one clean stroke.*

*The headless body collapsed to the ground, motionless. There was no blood. But seconds later, the black creature began to wiggle from the woman's open neck and began crawling straight toward him.*

*He had seen enough. He turned and fled, running fast and hard away from the clearing. He ran and he ran, and never looked back for fear that he might see something snaking its way after him through the pine needles. The forest became a blur of movement around him and his chest pounded and burned.*

*But he did not stop. Until …*

# 16

At the next stop, a cold wind followed the students aboard.

Jaden shivered.

"Told you that hoodie was crazy," Bill reminded him, tucked snugly in his own oversized winter jacket.

"We wouldn't be so cold if we sat in back, away from the door," Jaden said.

"But then we wouldn't be able to talk to Peg," Bill said, leaning forward in his seat so that his head was next to the bus driver's.

"Flattery will get you nowhere ... but school," Peg said, chuckling a bit at her own wit.

"You actually read those?" Bill asked, gesturing to a book that rested beside Peg. It was a well-leafed paperback with a fair-haired, full-muscled pirate on the cover.

"Don't knock it till you try it," Peg said.

"Let me see," Jaden said reaching forward, as Peg reluctantly passed back the paperback.

Jaden laughed.

"*Death on the High Seas*. You gotta be kidding me."

"It's romantic," she said.

"You smoke, Peg?" Bill asked eyeing the pack of cigarettes that had been hidden beneath the book.

"Yes," she said. "You shouldn't, though."

"When a woman has lost her way," Jaden began reading aloud from the back-cover summary, "only one man can lead her back ... one kiss at a time."

Jaden handed the book back.

"Sounds like your dad, Bill."

Peg laughed so hard, she nearly choked.

# 17

*… he broke through the forest and out onto a stretch of road. A car beeped and almost hit him, swerving as he dived aside. Again the car blared its horn and sped away.*

*The boy stood and brushed himself off. He was now standing in the center of a straight stretch of paved road. It was black with two yellow lines running down the middle. The dense trees of the forest on either side stretched as far as the eye could see.*

*It was quiet now that the car had passed. The trees were still. It began to rain.*

*He looked up at the sky and frowned. Then he looked to his left, then to his right, and after a moment decided on one direction and began to walk down the road.*

*The rain fell harder and harder, and it wasn't long before the boy found himself once more soaked right through to the skin. It was a cold rain and he was shivering. He could not brush the water from his eyes fast enough. The sky was growing ever darker. It would soon be night, and the boy did not know where he was or where he was going. But he kept walking, hoping to find the answer.*

*Instinctively, he turned his head to look behind him, and saw two headlights coming toward him through the sheets of rain. The boy stepped to the side of the road and watched as the lights drew closer, until the large truck they were attached to loomed into sight. It was a long truck, one with many tires, and as it neared, it began to slow, until finally, with a grunt of shifted gears, the truck rolled to a stop and a window lowered.*

*"Caught yourself in a bit of a downpour, huh?" said the man behind the wheel.*

*The boy nodded but said nothing.*

*"You want a lift? I can take you as far as Joe's if you like."*

*For a moment, the boy just stood in the rain. He saw a large brown dog pop into view beside the man.*

*"Get down, Tabby!" the man said. "It's just a kid, not a deer. Down."*

*The man turned back to him.*

*"So, what's it gonna be, fella? Ride or no?"*

*The boy nodded and clambered into the cab. Immediately, the dog was on him, sniffing and licking, wagging its tail furiously.*

*"Tabby, back! Get off him!" the man scolded with a smile. "She loves new people. The more the merrier, as far as she's concerned. Tabby, no! Just pat her some and she'll leave you alone."*

*The boy did just that but this only seemed to further encourage Tabby's affection. The man smiled wide and brought the truck back to gear and they began to roll forward. When they were full going the man offered a hand.*

*"Names Carl, but you can call me Johnny Cash," the man said. "Everyone else does."*

*The boy took his hand and they shook.*

*"Got a name?" Carl asked.*

*The boy remained silent, still trying to comprehend his ever-changing situation. Puzzled, Carl eyed him.*

*"You from around here?" he asked.*

*"No."*

*Carl nodded.*

*"Probably shouldn't be walking these back roads alone," he said. "Especially come night. Got a bike?"*

*"No."*

*Again, Carl looked him over.*

*"You out playing cowboys and Indians with your friends?"*

*The boy was silent.*

*"That thing for real?" Carl said, pointing to the boy's katana.*

*"Yes," the boy replied.*

*"Your parents know you got something like that?" Carl asked in a tone of knowing humor. "Probably don't, huh?"*

*The windshield wipers sloshed the rain away rhythmically, back and forth.*

*"How old are you, if you don't mind my asking?" Carl said.*

*"Fourteen, I think," the boy replied.*

*"You think?" Carl said, then paused. "You're not one of those runaways, are you?"*

*The boy patted the dog with one hand and then reached up and pushed the hair from his eyes.*

*Carl eyed him for a long moment, then shifted his eyes back onto the road. The boy peered ahead out the window and saw lights. He made out the words on the glowing sign just as they passed Joe's One Stop.*

*They were traveling fairly fast now.*

*"You got a girlfriend?" Carl asked.*

*Again, the boy did not answer.*

*"Where you staying tonight?"*

*Silence.*

*"Cat got your tongue?" Carl said, his tone now different than before. "You could stay with me … I mean, just for the night … if you got nowhere to go, I mean."*

*The boy remained silent.*

*"I got a cot in the back," Carl said. "Not much room, but I'm sure I could squeeze ya in."*

*He reached out and rested his hand on the boy's leg.*

*"You can let me out anytime now," the boy said. "This is where I need to be."*

*Carl smiled again, but it was no longer a friendly smile. This time, it was a smile caused by unspoken thoughts and plans. The man pulled back his hand and rested it on his own lap.*

*The boy's jaw tightened. He sat rigid.*

*"I'll show you where ya need to be," Carl said.*

*He reached over and grabbed the back of the boy's head, and tried to bring him over. The boy pulled away and slapped the man's hand away.*

*"Stay away from me!" he shouted.*

*"Oh, you wanna roughhouse, huh?" Carl said, again reaching out.*

*The boy spun himself sideways in his seat and kicked out with his feet, which connected hard with the side of Carl's head. He cursed, and the dog jumped and barked. Suddenly the truck was swerving down the slick road. Carl pumped the brakes and there was a loud screeching sound. The sudden jolt threw the boy forward in the cab and smashed him sideways through the windshield.*

# 18

"See you boys," Peg said as she watched them climb down the steps to the slightly colder world outside. It was windy, and Jaden and Bill walked quickly and silently, heads down, toward the school, passing a few school janitors who were salting the main walkway. Once inside, Jaden lowered his hood and shivered.

"Ahh … warmth," he said.

They turned down the hallway and walked on. Jaden sneezed.

"Envy," Bill said.

"Huh?"

"I envy you."

"Why?"

"You sneezed."

"So?"

"I heard that sneezing is like one-fifteenth of an orgasm. Your just got lucky. A little, anyway."

"What are you talking about?" Jaden said. "Where did you hear this?"

"On TV. It was on some show or something."

Jaden wiped his nose with his sleeve.

"I don't think my sneezes feel anything like an orgasm," he said. "Not even one-fifteenth. I hate sneezing."

"That's because you haven't been laid yet."

"What does that have to do with anything?"

"Everything."

"Well, maybe if I stole more porno magazines, I'd know better."

"Maybe," Bill said, barely hiding his smile.

# 19

*The boy smashed into a wall and fell to the floor in an upside-down heap. He lay there for a few moments with his legs bent above him, his mind once again trying to catch up. Soon, the initial feeling of disorientation began to fade, although not entirely. The boy brought his legs down, and pieces of glass came with them, falling all around him. He sat straight against the wall, with one hand pressed to his temple, and looked around.*

*He was sitting in a small room about the size of a closet, with a small toilet bowl and sink in front of him. Above the sink was the mirror through which he had crashed, but there was no hole to another place. No truck. Only gray paneling surrounded by what remained of the glass.*

*The boy noticed a shard of glass stuck in his palm and felt the pain that came with it. He winced as he pulled the glass out and began to bleed. He climbed to his feet on shaky legs and stood before the sink. He reached for the faucet, then stopped, recalling his last encounter with a faucet. Slowly, he reached for the faucet and turned it; thankfully, only water flowed from it.*

*The boy washed the blood away, then cupped his hands and brought a large handful of water to his face. Then another, and drank. He drank until he was no longer thirsty.*

*He turned the faucet off and looked at what was left of the mirror. One bottom corner still had a sizable piece of glass intact. He could see that his nose and cheeks were scratched, and he bled freely from a small gash just above his eye. There were some glass fragments in his hair.*

*He closed his eyes and shook the glass from his hair, then looked again into the mirror and frowned. He reached out and touched the wall behind the mirror. It was solid and cold. He lowered his hand and sighed deeply.*

*His katana lay on the floor in the glass. When he squatted to pick it up, he heard the low humming sound, which seemed to be coming from all around him. He turned and saw that the wall he had smashed into had a door. He took its handle and turned it, gripping the katana in his other hand.*

*The door opened into a dark, narrow hallway where the humming was much louder and more defined. It sounded mechanical. A single dark curtain hung in front of him, blocking his view beyond.*

*When he swept it aside, he saw dozens of seats lining either side of the aisle in which he now stood. The seats were empty. Suddenly, he realized he was moving, and moving fast.*

*The boy stepped forward slowly and cautiously. He paused, then slipped between seats and made his way to a window and pulled open the small curtain. And he saw that he was indeed moving—the world outside whipping past in a blur of white mist, and for the first time, he could hear the faint rattle of the tracks on the rails below.*

*Then he heard the whistle of the train he was now on.*

*He stepped back into the main aisle and made his way past row after row of empty seats, as a soft glow from above illuminated the area in a dull light. The boy walked on, looking to his left and right, his eyes searching and his ears listening. But all he could hear was the humming.*

*He made his way to the end of the aisle and swept aside another curtain to reveal another space identical to the one he had just left. He continued on, this time faster than before, past the many empty seats, until he reached another curtain—which led to another aisle leading down the center of rows of empty seats. At its far end, he could see another familiar, dark curtain.*

*The boy swallowed hard, took a deep breath, and began to jog down the aisle. He reached the curtain and brushed it aside, only to find yet another identical space. Again, he raced forward, his sandaled feet pounding down the carpeted aisle. This time, he ran through the curtain at the far end, then through another, and another, past row after row of empty seats. He continued on until the space around him was nothing more than a blur of motion. He withdrew his katana and cut through the next curtain as he passed, and then the next and then the next.*

*Finally, he stopped and let out an angry scream. His chest heaved as he gasped for air. His eyes narrowed; the curtain before him stood defiant, waiting.*

*The boy swept it aside, and his eyes widened.*

*This time, there was something new. It was the same rows of seats on either side of the middle aisle, but he could see a small cage sitting in the center of the aisle. The boy made his way to the cage, which he could see was empty. It had a small hinged door on the side, which was open. There was a string attached to the door that led away, down the aisle and under the next curtain.*

*The boy squatted down, took the string in his hand, and pulled. There was nothing but slack. He stood and swept aside the curtain, and saw that the string kept going all the way down the next aisle and under the next curtain.*

*He followed the string through countless aisles and countless curtains, until finally, he stopped. By now, he was sweaty and exhausted. And he finally plopped down in a seat and sat there staring at the string and the curtain before him.*

*He cursed.*

*Suddenly, the string moved and jerked as though it had been tugged.*

*The boy sprang from his seat and watched the string, waiting for more movement. But none came. He slowly made his way to the next curtain and pulled it aside, only to find another aisle and more empty seats. This time, however, the string disappeared underneath a door at the far end.*

*The boy froze, startled at the sight of something different than the countless curtains he had just passed. He inched forward to the door. It was a simple wooden door, thick and ajar. The string disappeared into the darkness on the other side. He took a few deep breaths and pushed the heavy door open.*

*On the other side was a small cabin filled with what appeared to be thousands of small beeping, glowing lights and dials and gauges. There were two seats directly ahead, and a large window beyond them, through which the boy could see an open expanse of tracks, just visible through the dense fog. As he stared, he was startled by a sound coming from the seats in front of him. He noticed the string he had been following twirled along the floor and up onto one of the seats.*

*He stepped forward and looked down over the back of the seat.*

*There was a little black monkey.*

*The animal wore an oversized conductor's hat. The monkey stood on its hind legs and leaned forward, clutching a pair of levers attached to the console of lights. He was carefully moving them forward and backward, as if he were driving the train. The string was attached to the monkey's tail in a tight knot.*

*The boy stared in disbelief. Finally, the monkey tilted its head and looked up at him.*

*"Eep?" it said.*

*Then the monkey turned back, and resumed its task.*

*The boy looked away from the monkey and out the window. The misty fog had lifted some, and now the boy could see the edge of a cliff in the distance. They were racing toward it, and their speed was increasing.*

*One random dial among the thousands began to beep louder then the rest. The monkey screeched and let go of the levers, and began to claw at the dial, then started biting it. Suddenly, the train surged and the boy felt himself falling forward. He grabbed the back of the seat to keep his balance. Again the monkey screeched and was once more back to the levers, now jerking them frantically back and forth.*

*The cliff loomed directly ahead, drawing much closer now. The monkey chirped contently.*

*The boy stepped back from the seat, unable to take his eyes off the approaching cliff and the tracks that ended at its edge. He reached past the monkey and took hold of the levers and tried to work them, but the moment he touched them he realized that, in fact, the levers were not actually working components. They were merely for show, as useless as sticks stuck in a couple of cup holders.*

*The monkey screeched and snatched the levers from the boy, and began to pump them dramatically.*

*"Eep!"*

*The boy watched this scene of madness for a moment more before he turned and fled. He ran down the aisle and through the curtain, and kept on running. Another aisle, then another, and then he could just hear the monkey screeching again and felt the train lurch. The boy lost his balance and fell hard into a seat. Suddenly, there was a terrible grinding sound and the aisle slanted sharply. The boy was thrown backward, and grasped a seat.*

*Loud, ringing alarms sounded from everywhere, and suddenly the ceiling seemed to explode. The boy fell forward and for a moment felt as though he were weightless. Then he hit the floor and slid down the aisle, trying desperately to grab a seat. But he couldn't, and he tumbled through the red curtain.*

# 20

The cafeteria was mostly empty when they arrived, with only a few groups scattered here and there. Bill made his way to the breakfast line as Jaden sat down at a table and waited. A few moments later, Bill returned with a tray of food. He sat, peeled the top off his cereal box, and folded open his milk. He began to pour.

"You want that?" Bill said, nodding toward the muffin on his tray.

"You don't?" Jaden said.

"They were out of blueberry. That's banana nut."

Jaden stared at the muffin for a moment, then reached over and took it.

"What's wrong with banana nut?" he asked.

"Nothing," Bill said as he took in a mouthful of cereal. "I just don't like the nuts."

"That's not what I hear," he said, sniffing at the muffin.

"Too easy," Bill said as he reached for his orange juice.

"Smells okay."

"Eat it."

Jaden stared thoughtfully at the muffin in his hand.

"I don't think I've ever had banana nut before,"

"Try it. Maybe you'll love it. I know how you love the nuts. Ha."

Jaden feigned laughter.

"Maybe …"

Jaden brought the muffin to his mouth and took a tiny bite.

He paused.

"So?" Bill asked.

"I don't think I like banana nut."

"Join the club."

"Tastes kinda funky. Pasty. Oily."

"Toss it."

"Maybe it's just a bad batch."

"Or someone peed in it."

The door to the cafeteria opened, and both boys glanced to see who had entered.

"Give it to Clarence," Bill said.

# 21

*As the red curtain slid aside, a bull charged forward, its long horns lowering for attack.*

*The boy quickly dove away just as the bull barreled past. The boy rose to his feet from the dirt and unsheathed his katana as the bull circled around and came back again, snorting angrily. Again, its horns lowered and the boy stood still, waiting till the last possible second before lashing out with the blade.*

*He finally lashed out as he jumped aside, severing the bull's legs. The animal crashed and crumpled forward in a furious heap of dust and dirt, writhing in agony, its back legs kicking wildly as blood spurted from its front two.*

*The boy stood and eyed the bull, then looked at his new surroundings. He was standing in an open arena with a thousand empty seats; he and the bull appeared to be alone.*

*The bull moaned and slumped awkwardly on its side. The boy came forward and put the animal out of its misery with a swift stab of the katana.*

*He took a deep breath and wiped the hair from his eyes. It was daytime, and the bright blue sky above was dotted with puffy clouds. The boy turned in a small circle and saw the opening at the far end of the arena. After one last glance at the dead animal, the boy resheathed his katana and began to walk across the arena toward the opening. As he drew nearer, he saw that the opening led into a dark tunnel, with a pinprick of light at its far end.*

*The boy twisted his mouth, took another breath, and then walked into the tunnel.*

# 22

"Hey, guys."

"Hey, Clarence," Jaden said.

Bill, whose mouth was full of food, nodded.

"What's with the big smile?" Jaden asked.

"That noticeable?" Clarence replied.

"What, did Darth Vader finally marry Mr. Spock?" Bill said.

Clarence stared.

"I'm not even going to dignify that with a response," he said.

Clarence put down his heavy book bag and sat down. He was a short boy with wavy red hair, glasses, and a mouth full of braces.

"So?" Jaden prodded.

Clarence's smile grew. He pointed to his bag.

"Fourth period, I'm going to show you something you're not gonna believe. You'll be electrified."

"What is it? What have you got?"

Clarence shook his head.

"Fourth period," he insisted.

"Can you at least give me a hint?"

"All right," Clarence said, hesitating for a moment. "It has to do with—"

"Dorkdom," Bill interrupted.

"Ignore him," Jaden said. "Now, what?"

"It has to do with … a certain superhero."

"What superhero?"

"Fourth period," Clarence said.

"Whoooo," Bill said sarcastically as though he were spooked. "The plot thickens!"

Clarence took his bag off the table and placed it on the floor.

"Why do you carry that thing around all day, anyway?" Bill asked.

"My bag? All my books are in it."

"Duh. I mean, why not put them in your locker? What does that thing weigh, like fifty pounds?"

"It's not *that* heavy. Besides, I don't use my locker."

"What do you mean you don't use your locker?"

"I don't use it."

"Why?"

Clarence threw Jaden a quick glance.

"I just don't."

Bill took in another mouthful of cereal and shook his head.

"You should at least get a different bag so you can wear it over both shoulders," he said. "I bet when you're older, one side of your body is gonna be bigger than the other. You'll be deformed."

"Will not," Clarence shot back. "That's the dumbest thing I've ever heard."

"Okay, we'll see. But I'll bet you fifty bucks by the time you're a senior, you'll already be walking with a limp."

"You can be really retarded sometimes, you know that?" Clarence said, and looked to Jaden as though he had to agree.

"Here, try this," Bill said, offering the muffin to Clarence.

# 23

*About halfway through the tunnel, the ground beneath his feet transformed from dirt to wooden planks, and the boy could just make out the parallel rails on either side. He was now on railroad tracks.*

*He stopped and looked back. He saw only darkness; the daylight from which he had come was gone.*

*He turned back and kept walking. The pin prick of light had grown to a fist size hole, and the boy quickened his pace. He soon reached the end of the tunnel and stepped out into the bright light of day. It was brighter than even moments, during the encounter with the bull.*

*Suddenly, he heard a blaring train whistle. Turning around, he saw a train barreled through the opening toward him. He jumped from the tracks just before the train whizzed by.*

*It was not a long train—only five cars—and it soon disappeared from sight around a bend. The boy just sat there beside the tracks, breathing hard, taking in all that had just happened. He could make no sense of it. Just then, he felt a sharp, throbbing pain in his temple. The boy touched the side of his head and felt the pain worsen.*

*He stood, brushed himself off, and readjusted his katana around his shoulder. Then he stepped back onto the tracks and began walking in the same direction as the train, often checking over his shoulder again and again, until he was far enough away not to worry.*

*The tracks curved around a sharp bend. On one side was a sheer cliff that dropped into a dry canyon. On the other side was a rock wall. The boy took the bend with caution, wary of another train barreling at him from the opposite direction. Finally, the boy stopped dead.*

*He saw two little girls playing on the tracks. They were younger than him and dressed in identical school outfits: white tops with matching checkered skirts. They both wore long, white socks that ran high on their legs, and matching black shoes that caught the suns rays and sparkled as though aflame. They were jumping rope, one on each rail, their black ponytails bouncing.*

*"Hello …" the boy said and when they did not respond he raised his voice. "Hello?"*

*They turned to him. They were identical twins.*

*"Hi," they said together, cheerfully, not bothering to stop jumping.*

*"What are you doing here?" the boy asked. "Where are we? Who are you?"*

*The girls eyed each other and giggled, then turned away from him. Together they began to skip rope down the rails, leaving him behind.*

*"Hey wait," he said, trotting ahead to catch up. "Listen to me. I need your help. I need you to help me. I need you to answer me."*

*They again giggled.*

*He let out a tired breath.*

*"I'm lost," he said. "I can't find my way. Please ... if you could just—"*

*"Cute boys shouldn't travel alone," they said in unison. "It can be dangerous for cute boys. Very dangerous."*

*"It is dangerous," he agreed. "But if you would—"*

*"The train's coming again," they said together. "We can feel it."*

*"Then we should leave these tracks," the boy replied. "Let's go. You could bring me to your parents. You could—"*

*His words were suddenly drowned out by the sound of the train whistle. He could feel the tracks trembling beneath him.*

*"It's close now," they said.*

*"You should really get off the rails," he said. "You—"*

*Again, the whistle covered his words with its high-pitched shriek. The tracks beneath his feet shook violently. The boy turned back just as the train came into view around the bend. It was black and twice as big as the other train. Sparks shot from the rails beneath it as it barreled forward. He turned back to the girls.*

*"Hey!" he shouted. "Get off the tracks! It's coming! Look its coming!"*

*They just giggled.*

*The boy looked back and saw the train racing forward. It would reach them in seconds.*

*"Get off! Get off! Get off!" he yelled, racing toward the girls.*

*He made to grab one girl but she would not budge. He grabbed her by the arm and pulled, but her flesh merely tore away, like a glove being pulled off of a hand, and the boy fell backward onto the tracks. He started to get up, but he realized it was too late; the train was almost upon him. He screamed and lay as flat as he could on the tracks. Just before the train hit the girls, he could hear them giggling.*

*The train passed over him; it was so close, he could reach up slightly and touch it. He squeezed shut his eyes and turned his head away. The sound was deafening. The wheels were grinding the rails just inches away, and sparks were spitting into his face. And then, just as quickly as it had come, it was over. The train had passed and its whistle sounded, holding its note as it faded into the distance.*

*The boy lay there, shuddering with fear, but finally gathered the courage to open his eyes. He sat up …*

# 24

The first bell rang, and the boys all got up from the table and wandered out of the cafeteria.

"See you guys later," Clarence said as he trudged off with his cumbersome book bag slung over one shoulder.

"Weirdo," Bill muttered as he watched him leave. "He really will be deformed. Not that it'd change anything."

"You're cruel," Jaden said with a grin. "He just doesn't know how to work a combination lock."

"Huh?"

"Clarence. His locker—he can't open it."

"Are you kidding?"

"He asked me to teach him like a thousand times, and I tried, but he could never get it."

"What's to get?"

"He gets confused with the spinning left and right stuff."

Bill sighed.

"I thought he was Mr. Brainiac."

"Oh, he's smart, trust me. Probably too smart. But …"

"Can't be that smart," Bill said. "He ate that muffin, didn't he?"

# 25

*... and saw that he was no longer on the tracks.*

*"No," he whispered in disbelief. "Please ... stop this."*

*Now he was sitting in a small boat. The blue glint of the open sea in all directions was blinding. The waves ebbed and fell rhythmically. Suddenly, the sky opened up and a downpour fell upon him.*

*But it was not rain. It was red and warm, and smelled of metal. It was blood.*

*Within moments, he was soaked through his clothes, and the downpour wasn't stopping. It intensified until the sky had taken on the bluish-purple color of a deep bruise. A quick flash of lightning lit up the sky and sea. Thunder boomed.*

*Then the first hailstone splashed down just a few feet away. The boy gasped. Another hailstone hit, this time closer, then another and another. The boy looked around frantically, but the boat lay empty. No sail, no oars—nothing at all. Just him.*

*Another hailstone landed in the boat with a thud, and broke apart into a thousand tiny balls of red, crystallized ice, rocking the boat in its wake. Thunder made the boat shudder even more. Suddenly, a wave broke hard against the boat, nearly tipping it, and splashed a mist of salty spray into the air.*

*The boy lost his balance and toppled head-first to the boat's bottom. Before he could lift himself, a large hailstone struck him in the back, right between the shoulders. As he yelled out in pain, another struck him in the lower back and another in the leg. Another hit him in the back of the head like a punch.*

*Furious, he spun around and climbed to his feet, and here lifted his head to the dark sky. He cursed the heavens as blood and hail showered down upon him; his hair was plastered wet and crimson. The boy pulled his katana and attempted to fend off the hail, managing to cut away a huge one before it hit him. But he couldn't get them all.*

*One more whipped down like a comet and struck the boy in the face. He was thrown back and tripped, and tumbled off the boat and into the sea.*

# 26

Jaden had just sat down at his desk when second bell sounded. The class was full of students milling about, talking and laughing.

"Why do you hang around him anyway?" Bill asked.

"Who?" Jaden said, turning sideways in his seat to face Bill, who was seated behind him.

"Clarence. He's a total geek."

"Everyone's a geek. *I'm* a geek."

"Not like him. He's an uber-geek. All he's missing is the suspenders."

"He's all right."

A girl a few seats up from them laughed, and both boys eyed her. Bill looked at Jaden and pursed his lips.

"You wish," Jaden said.

"I know," Bill said confidently, eyes drifting back to her. "Just a matter of time."

"Till what, hell freezes over?"

Bill feigned laughter.

"Hold your nose," Bill said looking toward the door.

Just then the teacher, Mr. Olack, entered the classroom, and the students headed for their assigned seats.

"All right, all right," Mr. Olack said. "Settle down. Settle down."

He propped his briefcase on his desk, flipped it open, and took out a couple books.

Bill leaned forward a little in his seat and whispered the sounds of a seagull, quickly followed by the sound of a ringing buoy.

Jaden smiled.

"Quiet please. Everyone, quiet."

The voices softened to a murmur, then fell silent.

Mr. Olack pulled a piece of paper from his case and stepped in front of his desk.

"Halaway."

"Here," said a girl in the first seat.

"Hallorain."

"Here."

"Hancock."

"Here."

There came a knock on the door.

"Excuse me," said a stout man in a suit and tie, "sorry to interrupt."

Mr. Olack stepped out into the hall to talk to him.

"Looks like the stink police finally got their man," Bill whispered.

Jaden snickered.

Mr. Olack came back in. "Jaden, would you please?" he said, motioning toward the door.

"Me?" Jaden said pointing to himself.

Mr. Olack nodded.

Jaden stood and began to make his way to the front of the room.

"Bring your belongings," Mr. Olack said.

Jaden gathered up his book bag and left the room. In the hallway, the man in the suit and tie was waiting for him.

"Hello, my name's Mr. Devalley. I'm a guidance counselor," he said, extending his hand. "It's nice to meet you, Jaden."

The two shook hands.

"If you don't mind, I'd like to speak to you for a few moments," he said. "It won't be long. I'll get you back to class in a flash. Okay?"

"Sure."

"Then if you could accompany me to my office."

# 27

*He tried to resurface, but found that he was now enclosed in an underwater passage.*

*The boy swam through the watery depths of the passage, his arms and fingers reaching, searching for a way out. He continued to make his way forward until the very passage began to close in around him.*

*He could now feel the tunnel around him, and a terrible pang of claustrophobia gripped him, a swell of panic that threatened to take him as air bubbles escaped his mouth in a spray. Somehow he managed to fight off his fear and continued onward, even as he felt the passage tighten around his shoulders. He swam on, legs kicking and hips swiveling, his arms outstretched before him like a drill. The passage continued to shrink.*

*It was as dark as the deepest, blackest hole, and the boy closed his eyes. He wiggled and squirmed forward. There was little he could do now. The last few feet of the tunnel funneled down to a fist-sized hole, and the boy found himself trapped, stuck, and unable to move.*

*He had reached a dead end.*

*He screamed, and air bubbles left him with his muffled, distorted voice. He desperately stuck his hand through the tiny opening, reaching and thrashing. Suddenly, he felt something—or the lack of something. His hand was in dry air, free of the water.*

*He groped frantically, reaching his arm through the hole all the way to the elbow. His fingers felt something cool and dry: an edge of some kind, something to grip. He clenched his fingers around this dry edge and tried with all his might to pull himself through. But he couldn't. The hole was solid and would not give.*

*He screamed again, the last of his breath escaping him, and reached forward with his other hand in a desperate attempt to squeeze it through the opening. At first, he could not, but he kept at it. He could feel the skin on his wrists tearing, but could also feel his other hand finally slipping through the opening. He wiggled wildly, pushing and squirming and thrashing, and his other hand somehow squeezed through the opening and felt air, and then the cool edge.*

*The boy clenched all ten of his fingers, gripping and straining, his muscles tense and throbbing. He pulled and pulled, even as his lungs burned like fire. He swallowed his first gulp of water and he could hear his heartbeat in his ears, pounding violently as he pulled again and again.*

*Finally, he broke through the hole …*

# 28

The office was very small and very hot. Mr. Devalley sat down behind his desk, which occupied most of the room's space, and offered the only other seat to Jaden.

Jaden sat.

Mr. Devalley began to type away at his computer and for a few moments Jaden waited, twisting his hoodie's drawstring between his fingers.

"Ah, here we go," Mr. Devalley said as he sat straight and looked at Jaden, and then back at the screen. "Do you know why you are here, Jaden?"

"No."

"Well, it would appear that your attendance as of late has been—how shall I say—spotty."

He looked at Jaden for a moment, then shifted his eyes back to the screen.

"You've missed four days this week … two last week … three the week before that."

He looked up. "That sound about right?"

"I guess," Jaden mumbled.

Mr. Devalley nodded.

"And there have been other days, too, stretching back to the start of the term. I'd say you've missed about a good quarter of this term thus far."

Jaden sat silent.

"Have you been sick?"

"I suppose."

"I'm only asking because that's what all your notes from home have said."

He again eyed Jaden, obviously fishing for some clues.

"So, do you feel better now?" he asked.

"I guess so," Jaden replied.

"And you were out this week thus far because you were sick again?"

"Yeah. I've got another note in my bag," Jaden replied as he started to search for the note. "I was gonna give it to Mr. Olack but—"

"But I came along," Mr. Devalley interrupted.

Jaden nodded.

"Well, it's part of my job to keep track of attendance here at Samrye High. So you could just give that note to me, I suppose. It's where it'll end up anyway."

Jaden found the note and handed it to Mr. Devalley, who unfolded it and read it intently, as though it were a paragraph long instead of a mere sentence.

"I see ..." he said, rubbing his chin.

Mr. Devalley refolded the note and placed it on his desk, then leaned back. His chair creaked with his weight. He folded his hands on his lap and stared squarely at Jaden.

"You know, when a student misses a certain number of days, it tends to send up a red flag of sorts," he said. "And that's when I'm called into action. You see?"

Jaden nodded.

"There are all kinds of students at this school. The good, the bad ... the ugly."

Mr. Devalley grinned a toothy grin at his little joke.

"Though I believe that you fall under the good, Jaden ..." he said, pausing for effect, "I've talked to most of your teachers and they all agree. You're a good student. Good grades, good manners—good all around. Everyone I've spoken to has had nothing but good things to say of you.

He paused again.

"Except for this last term," he continued. "It seems here is where your grades, at least, went from good to somewhat bad. And of course, there's the matter of your attendance."

There was a moment of silence.

"Look, I know what you're thinking," Mr. Devalley said. "You're thinking I'm trying to be some kind of hammer here. But that's not the case. Not at all. In fact, most students who get to know me find I'm a pretty okay guy. I may be older than you, but I can still smell what the Rock is cooking."

And here he raised his eyebrow high and mimicking. Jaden just stared.

"Look, what I'm trying to say is that just because I'm sitting on this side of the desk, it doesn't mean I don't understand what a kid your age goes through," Mr. Devalley said. "Hell, school's tough. It's demanding, it's annoying. But so is life. And 90 percent of life is just showing up, you know?"

He sighed sympathetically.

"I didn't necessarily want to come to work today, but I did," he continued. "And I know you're thinking: well, I get paid to be here, and that's true. But let me ask you this Jaden: would you come to school more often if you were being paid?"

Jaden shrugged.

"I'm just trying to understand."

Mr. Devalley paused again.

"So, why have we *really* been missing all this school Jaden?" he asked. "Is it just playing hooky?"

"I've got notes."

"And I think we both know how valid those are, don't we?"

"I don't know what you mean."

Mr. Devalley smiled. "Do your parents know?"

"Know what?"

"That you've been skipping?"

"What do the notes say?"

"They say you were sick," Mr. Devalley replied, with an even wider grin.

Jaden shrugged as if that should be enough.

"Were you sick, Jaden?" he asked pointedly, yet playfully.

They stared at each other. Suddenly, the bell sounded then.

Mr. Devalley leaned forward.

"Class begins," he said as he typed a few things. "I believe we're pretty much through here."

Jaden stood up and slung his bag over his shoulder. He opened the door and was just stepping out when Mr. Devalley stopped him.

"Jaden," he said, not bothering to look up from his computer monitor. "I'm going to have to call your parents if you miss another day. Just a warning."

Jaden stared at the man in the tiny hot office. Then he turned and left.

# 29

*... and burst out into the open air.*

*He gasped deeply, and began to cough and sputter. He spat and took more deep breaths. It was only after he finally regained his breath that he realized he was hanging halfway out of a toilet.*

*The toilet was dirty. Its natural white finish had grayed with time and use. The boy pulled himself out and lay on the floor in a wet, heap. Around him, the room in which he now found himself was misty and wet, with gray tiled floors and walls slick with moisture. The air was thick with steam. Everything was illuminated by a dim, flickering light high in the ceiling above. The only sound was that of dripping.*

*The boy pushed himself up to a sitting position and pulled his legs in close, hugging his knees and shivering. His mop of blond hair hung down in his face, and his wet clothes felt as heavy as concrete. He took long deep breaths, and muttered under his breath. He heard the sudden, distant, sounds of brayed laughter coming from somewhere, followed closely by a shout of anguish. His hand instinctively went to the hilt of his katana and clutched.*

*He listened, but now there was only silence, except for the dripping.*

*The boy stood still, listening. The space he was in was walled on all sides except for one, and he slowly made his way to this opening and peeked cautiously around the corner. His eyes widened as he saw a large, misty shower room with more than a dozen shower heads sticking out the tops. A few shower heads were spraying hot water that swirled down into drains. And standing within these streams of water were naked women.*

*The boy swallowed hard and watched silently, unable to move.*

*One of the women glanced to her side and saw him. She was a large woman with wide legs and arms as thick as lumber. Her body rippled with bulging muscle. She eyed the boy without shock or surprise, and simply pushed back her soapy hair.*

*Then she grinned. She reached forward and twisted the knob, and her shower fell away. She placed the bar of soap she was holding in her large fist into a tiny space in the wall and turned to face the boy.*

*"Finally letting us have a little fun around here," she said in a lusty voice.*

*The other women in the shower noticed the boy, too, and one by one, they all ended their showers and faced him.*

*"What's your name kiddo?" the large woman asked with a slight purse of the lips.*

*The boy's mouth opened and closed without a word or sound.*

*"Cat got your tongue?" she asked.*

*"I—I'm not suppose to be h-here," he stammered, and took a step back. "I'm sorry I—"*

*"Don't be sorry," the woman replied with a crack of her knuckles. "I think you're exactly where you ought to be. Ain't he?"*

*The other women's eyes scanned him as though they were hungry wolves eyeing a pile of meat. A woman at the far end giggled softly.*

*After a moment of the women and the boy staring at each other, he turned and fled back into the space from which he came. He ran to the toilet and saw that it was just that, and no longer a passage to another place. Just a dirty porcelain hole meant to be shit in.*

*"Where you going, kiddo?" a woman's voice called out.*

*The boy whirled and saw the large woman standing just inside the space. The others were close behind her, watching intently.*

*"Stay away!" he pleaded, pulling his katana out in a deliberate sweep.*

*"Oh, now," the woman said in a soothing manor. "No need for any of that. You just put that there thing down and we can do a little talkin'. Just you and me."*

*The woman stepped forward.*

*"I said stay back!" the boy shouted, raising his katana and cutting the air before him as a warning. "Don't come near me! None of you!"*

*"Now, now, little kiddo. You just relax yourself."*

*The woman came forward yet again, arms flexing, eyes gleaming. Her pace quickened as she drew nearer. The boy cut out with his katana and severed most of the woman's fingers from her hands. She screamed as she backpedaled, her arms folding inward holding herself, and fell back against the far wall.*

*"He cut me! He cut me!" she shrieked. "The little whore cut me!"*

*The other women standing in the opening retreated and were gone. He could hear their wet footsteps on the tiled floor as they scurried away.*

*"Look what you did to me! Look at it!" the woman screamed.*

*She slid down to sit on the floor, holding her bloodied hands out before her.*

*"Look at 'em! Look!"*

*The boy took a wide birth around the woman and ran out of the room and back out to the showers. The other women weren't there.*

*"Come back here you!" she yelled. "Come back and gimme back my hands! Gimme back! Gimme back!"*

*Without hesitation, the boy ran through the showers and down a long, grimy, gray hallway. He could see a door on the far end, and once he reached it he grabbed the handle.*

*"Gimme back, you dirty little whore!" a distant voice called to him.*

*The boy turned the handle and opened the door …*

# 30

Jaden was the first student to enter the class.

"Hello, Jaden," Mrs. Willard said as he walked up the middle aisle toward his desk.

Mrs. Willard was quite old. She wore a gray one-piece dress, and her gray hair was usually rolled into a tight bun. Her hands shook as she talked.

"Hey," Jaden said softly as he took his seat.

Moments later, the other students began to file in. A rather chunky girl walked in, wearing too-tight black pants and a taxed black hoodie. Her hood was up, concealing most of her face, but Jaden could still see the pale skin, which looked even paler with the dark makeup around her eyes. Even from across the room he could see that her fingernails were painted black. As soon as she saw Jaden, her mouth formed an O. He waved. She waved eagerly as she took her seat on the other side of the class.

After she took attendance, Mrs. Willard talked at length about the reading assignment from the previous night. When she was finished talking about the homework, she instructed the students on their lab assignment.

"Same stations as yesterday," she said. "And remember class, be careful, or otherwise you might burn your own *Bun*sen."

She placed a hand on her backside and chuckled at her bit of wit, as did a few of the students who sat closest.

"Mrs. Willard?"

"Yes Jaden," she replied, as her hands shook and shook.

"I wasn't here yesterday. I don't have a station."

Mrs. Willard squinted.

"Um, yes, well, just group up with someone," she replied. "They'll catch you up."

The students began to rise from their seats and make their way to lab area in the back of the class. Jaden walked up to Gloria, who still had her hood covering her head.

"I'm your partner," he announced.

Gloria feigned shock, and the pair made their way to the back cabinets to begin gathering their supplies.

Without looking at him, Gloria said, "Two vaginas walk into a bar and ask for the usual. The bartender asks, 'What's the usual?' And the one vagina says, 'What we always get.' And the bartender says, 'What, once a month?'"

"That was lame," Jaden said, rolling his eyes.

"I know, but don't you just love it?"

"Not particularly."

"Funny, my mother nearly choked on her meatloaf when I told her."

Jaden cracked a slight smile.

"Ahh, now were talking," Gloria said. "So are you going to tell me why you look like there's never going to be another *Halloween* sequel or what?"

"I've just got a headache is all," Jaden replied with a sigh.

"Well, I've got something that will cheer you up."

He waited. Gloria stuck out her tongue and Jaden's eyes widened in surprise. Her tongue was now pierced.

"When did you get that?"

"Get what?"

"Seriously."

"Last Saturday. Of course, if we ever talked anymore, you'd already know that, wouldn't you?"

"Sorry."

"Are you?"

"No," Jaden shot back with a slight grin. "Who did it?"

"Moi," Gloria replied, pointing to herself.

"*You*? Are you kidding me?"

They made their way back to the workstation and began to sort and organize their supplies.

"No, I'm not kidding. And don't act too shocked, it's insulting. I'm not a child, you know."

"So how'd you do it?"

Gloria smiled mischievously. "Used one of my mother's sowing needles."

"You *what*? Didn't it hurt? I mean, aren't you supposed to use something to numb it or something?"

"I sucked on ice. Besides, it really doesn't hurt the way you're thinking. It's just like getting a shot."

"In your *tongue*," he reminded her.

"Okay, so maybe it hurt a little, but I ate a Creamsicle, and it felt better."

She turned on the Bunsen burner.

"I think you should let me do most of this," she said.

"I'm not arguing," he replied.

Gloria made a few adjustments and then began to fill a test tube with a clear colored liquid.

"Don't drink that," she said as though speaking to an infant.

"So it didn't hurt, huh?" Jaden asked.

"Nope."

"Not even a little?"

"Nope."

He looked at her unconvinced.

"All right," she admitted in a gush, "it hurt like hell and I cried, and nearly—*nearly*—peed my pants. Satisfied?"

"Not really. Aren't you worried about infection or something?"

"Infection?"

"Uh yeah ... did you even sterilize the needle?"

She stared back at him blankly.

Jaden sighed. "You're supposed to like cook it in boiling water before," he said.

"My tongue has been kinda sore all week," she said. "I've been feeling kinda sick too. But I just thought that was part of it."

"You may wanna get that checked out," he said. "Like immediately."

"Oh, my god. If my mom finds out, she'll kill me."

"Well, better *her* killing you then whatever it is you got going on in your mouth right now," Jaden said. "At least she'll make it quick and painless—you know, motherly love and all."

"There'll be no motherly love if she finds out," Gloria said. "Maybe if I just take it out ..."

"What, your tongue?"

"Shut up. Do you think that will fix it?"

"I'm no doctor."

"So you wouldn't recommend me drinking bleach then?"

"How about you just drink whatever it is you got cooking in that test tube."

They both eyed the boiling tube, whose liquid had now turned gray.

"It might make you into a superhero—a super serum—like Captain America," Jaden said.

"That or a freak like the Joker."

"Well, you've already got the makeup," he said, getting a playful punch to his arm in return.

# 31

*... and stepped into the room. It was a dojo.*

*The boy stood at the back of the room motionless. The dojo was filled with empty desks and chairs. At the front of the room was a large desk, and behind it stood a woman. She had her back to him and was writing on the blackboard. A late-afternoon light seeped through the far windows in the form of hazy light beams that swirled alive with the smallest pieces of discarded life, bright and dusty. On the wall, a large, old-fashioned clock ticked the seconds away.*

*Tick. Tick. Tick.*

*"Excuse me ... Ma'am?"*

*The woman did not acknowledge his presence. She continued to write.*

*He stepped forward.*

*"Hello?" he said as he took another step.*

*The woman ignored him. His eyes drifted to the words on the board. They read:*

> *He will have lost considerable weight ... arms thinner ... hip bones pointy ... and extremely weak ... thirsty ... throat and voice raspy ... his stomach will have shrunk ... and thus at first, very little food and even just water will be enough to make him feel bloated ... full ... he will be pale ... hair tangled ... knotty ... messy ... sunken cheeks ... bags under his eyes ...*

*The boy stopped. He stared at the woman's back.*

*"I need help," he said. "I—"*

*"I used to read old heavy hardcovers by window light," the woman said abruptly without turning to face him. "That was a good time, my childhood. The world was simple then. People were simple. Pleasures were simple. Problems were simple. Things have certainly changed since those days. The world has grown bigger, and with it, so have the pleasures and the problems. No longer is it safe to assume the good. People cannot be trusted the way they once could. It is impossible to know what really lurks in the minds of others these days. One has to always be on guard, at all hours, against evil holes and those who dig them. People have become mean and cruel and paranoid. No one is safe anymore. No one is spared the cruelties of this world. Anyone can slip and fall into despair and loss of hope."*

*The woman paused for a moment.*

*"But especially vulnerable are the children," she continued. "They are the weakest of all."*

*Finally, the woman turned to face the boy. She was very old. Her gray hair was pulled and pinned securely into a tight bun. Her face looked small and sunken, and was covered with deep wrinkles. Her mouth caved inward, cracked like a dried-out water hole, and her nose was perched, crooked, short, and ugly. Her fingers were sickly thin, and hung loosely from her kimono sleeves like broken sticks. Her eyes were black as coal.*

*For a long, uninterrupted moment, the old woman and the boy just stared at each other. Then movement outside the window caught their attention. A little girl was racing across the field back toward the school.*

*"At one time, a better time," the old woman began, "she would be running home to play with her friends and family till the sun tired and sunk behind the hills. But no, in this new world, who can possibly know who she runs to or from? Truly in a world where evil seems to pick and choose its victims at random, there is little anyone can do to prevent certain horrors."*

*The woman turned to the boy for a moment, then shifted her gaze back out the window. The little girl had come closer now. She wore a pretty yellow kimono that appeared to almost float as though her small, delicate, feet were not meant to touch the ground.*

*"It is the way of all the young ones," the old woman said. "They know little of the evils of the world, and they still move about as though all is peaceful and pleasant."*

*They both watched as the little girl suddenly knelt down among the green grass and wildflowers to adjust a sock or sandal. Then she was off again, right past the back windows, fluttering along as carefree as a butterfly.*

*"She comes back for her book," the old woman said, eyeing a desk with a single brown book on top of it.*

*Just then, the little girl entered the room from the same doorway the boy had come through. She saw the boy and stopped.*

*"It is all right, child," said the old woman. "Retrieve your book if you wish."*

*The girl hesitated for a moment, still eyeing the boy with the katana, as though he were a strange animal that she wasn't sure if she could trust. Then she made her way to her desk. The desk was at the front of the room and thus the little girl passed the old woman along the way. She took her book in her hands and paused to eye the strange boy again.*

*"Run along, child," the old woman said. "Run along."*

*The little girl nodded, clasped the book tight to her chest, and made her way back toward the door. But as she passed, the old woman suddenly grabbed the little girl by her hair. Before the girl could struggle or scream, the old woman smashed her face forward into the desk in front of them, splintering the wood in half.*

*The boy flinched and clasped the hilt of his katana.*

*The old woman pulled the little girl back and held her slumped body by the hair like a child's doll. The girl's face was a broken mask of crimson.*

*"You are crazy!" the boy said in barely more than a whisper.*

*"No," the old woman said, "the world is mad."*

*She lowered her mouth to the little girl's head and took a wide, chomping bite.*

*The boy pulled out his katana. The old woman dropped the little girl's lifeless body to the ground and looked up at the boy. Her mouth dripped of blood, flesh, and hair.*

*She smiled.*

*Then she began to come forward quickly, pushing desks out of the way as she did. The boy stepped back.*

*"Stay away from me!" he warned. "I have killed before! I will kill again!"*

*But the old woman didn't even flinch. She tossed a desk aside as though it were made of cardboard. The boy stepped back until he was finally backed up against a wall. The old woman tossed another desk aside and was nearly upon him. The boy raised his katana at the ready.*

*"Stay back!" he shouted.*

*But the woman came, and the boy lashed out with his blade. In one clean slice, he severed the old woman's head from her body. Blood sprayed from her open neck like a geyser, showering the room in a mist of red. For a moment, the old woman's body stood erect before finally collapsing lifelessly to the floor.*

*The boy leaned against the back wall, covered in blood, silent and still.*

*Finally, he resheathed his katana and went to the dojo door, which was shut. He eyed it for a moment, then turned away, picked up a chair, and threw it through the nearest window. He climbed up to the windowsill and without so much as a glance back, jumped out the window and into the grassy field and the light of day.*

# 32

The students were now recording notes in their lab journals. The Bunsen burner was off and the liquid in the test tube was cooling, and changing color again.

"So, how's your book coming along?" Gloria asked.

"It's not a book—just a story."

"Okay, so how's your *story* coming along then?"

"Fine."

"You don't sound so sure."

He sighed. "It's okay. I mean, it's not terrible, I think."

"What's it about again? A samurai kid going around killing people?"

"Something like that. Why are you suddenly interested in that all of a sudden?"

"I'm not. I'm just bored."

She smiled. "No seriously, what is it about?"

"Pretty much what you said, I guess."

"A samurai kid who kills people?"

"Yeah, sorta."

"What's his name?"

"Doesn't have one."

"Why not? Writer's block?"

She grinned.

"He doesn't remember."

"Amnesia?"

"Not really."

"What then?"

"He just can't because …"

"Because?"

"He's not ready to remember, I guess."

"You guess? Aren't you writing it? Shouldn't you know everything about him?"

"Not really. He's kinda a mystery to me sometimes," Jaden said. "It's better that way, I think."

"Listen to you, sounding all artsy-fartsy," Gloria shot back. "I like it. Hmmm … the boy with no name …"

She thought for a moment, then smiled.

"So is he cute?" she asked.

"Who?"

"This samurai kid. Big, dark, and handsome?"

Jaden grinned.

"Probably just the opposite."

"Small, pale, and ugly?" she said, scrunching her face. "Ewww."

Jaden shook his head.

"How old is he?"

"About fourteen, I guess."

She looked at him with puzzlement.

"He doesn't happen to have long blond hair, a cute pug nose, and wear baggy raver pants with a mile-long drawstring, does he?" she asked.

"Actually, he does have long blond hair and a cute pug nose, but, he wears hakima pants. He's a—"

"Samurai, right?" she interrupted. "He's not gay, is he?"

Jaden shrugged. "That hasn't really come up. So—"

"But it's to be assumed?"

"I guess I'll let the reader decide that kinda stuff for themselves."

Gloria paused for a moment.

"Have you told them yet?" she asked.

Jaden's pen stopped moving. He stared at his paper without a word. Finally, he shook his head silently.

A long few moments passed.

"So when do I receive the honor of reading this masterwork?" Gloria said, flipping her notebook shut and chewing on her pen. "You almost done or what?"

"I think I'm close," he replied. "But it's hard to tell."

"Why's that?"

"Haven't really come up with an ending yet."

"But you've got ideas?"

"Yeah, a few. But things don't usually end up the way you plan them to. Not mostly, anyway."

"Well, I want you to promise that I get to be the first to read it when you're done."

"I promise," he said with a nod.

"Promise what?" she asked with a grin and a raise of her eyebrows.

"That when I'm finished, you'll be one of the first to know."

"*The* first."

"Right."

"Class, tidy-time," Mrs. Willard interrupted with a clap of her shaking hands. "Finish what you're doing and start to clean up. Put everything away where you found it."

The students cleaned the beakers in the deep sink. As Gloria finished up what remained, Jaden gathered up the loose supplies and returned them to the back racks and cabinets. He had just opened the large cabinet door and was putting the instruments back inside when another boy came around.

"Long time no see," Joshua said.

Jaden placed a beaker in the back of a cabinet. He did not even glance at the other boy.

Joshua, who was a head taller than Jaden and wore a football jersey with the number 43 on it, sighed.

"Too good for football now?" he asked in a low sneer.

Jaden continued to ignore him.

"Coach said you're off the team, ya know," Joshua said in a mocking tone.

"I don't care," Jaden replied.

"I'll bet you don't," Joshua snapped. "You would've never played much anyway. You gotta have more than speed, ya know."

"Leave me alone, all right?"

"What's your problem?" Joshua asked, leaning close. "Faggot."

With that, he gave Jaden a sharp blow in the chest with his elbow. Jaden dropped the test tubes he was holding, and they shattered on the floor.

"Later," Joshua mouthed, stepping away as Mrs. Willard trembled her way across the classroom.

# 33

*The field was wide and long, and stretched far into the distance. When the boy looked over his shoulder, he was not the least bit surprised to see that the dojo was gone. It was replaced with more open space. No trees. No houses. Nothing.*

*Just grass.*

*The boy wiped the blood off of his face, took a deep breath, and began to walk toward the distant horizon.*

*The sun was making its downward descent, dipping from a scorched, orange sky, when the field came to an abrupt end at a cliff. The boy stepped closer and looked down. A deep canyon fell away to darkness. Across the way there was another cliff and another field, perhaps the same field, as though the very earth had been split between them. A long rope bridge stretched between the two cliffs.*

*The boy stepped to the bridge and looked across, pulling his katana out as he did. The bridge appeared old and worn, and swayed slightly in the soft breeze. The wood-planked bottom looked rotted in places, and he could see a few boards were missing here and there. At the center of the bridge sat a single silhouetted figure.*

*He swallowed and began to make his way across the bridge. When he was close enough to see the figure more clearly, he slowed.*

*"Hello?" the boy said guardedly.*

*The figure, which wore a long dark robe and hood, sat with its legs crossed and its head bowed, and did not speak or stir.*

*"May I—"*

*"You cannot pass," the figure said in a hollow voice that sounded as though it were spoken from the bottom of a well. "You are not yet ready."*

*"Why?" the boy asked. "What is this? What is going on here? Who are you?"*

*The man said nothing.*

*"I need to get past," the boy said after a moment, now growing agitated.*

*"I intend to meditate without further interruption," the figure said.*

*"You can meditate when I pass," the boy replied.*

*The figure raised his head and lowered his hood to face the boy for the first time. The boy blinked wordlessly.*

*The figure wore a dark mask fitted with tight, interlocking straps and buckles that were intertwined with his dark hair, sprouting through like a patch of wild weeds.*

*The eyes of the mask were of a dark and reflective material; the boy could see his reflection in them.*

*"You believe yourself brave, do you?" the figure asked.*

*"No," the boy replied. "I believe myself desperate. I'm lost and I need to get across this bridge."*

*"Why?"*

*The boy had no answer.*

*The dark robes billowed around the man and for a long moment, the two faced each other silently.*

*"Perhaps because you believe the answers you seek are awaiting you on the other side?"*

*"Maybe," the boy replied. "I don't know. I don't know anything about this place. And I don't want to."*

*"Do you fear me?" the other asked abruptly.*

*"Yes," the boy replied after a thoughtful pause.*

*"But you will overcome this fear if you must. You will act?"*

*The boy said nothing.*

*"Very well," said the other. "Then you should know boy—ronin boy—that I am without weapon."*

*The boy's eyes narrowed.*

*"Which does not make me defenseless," the figure added. "No, it does not. However, it does give you a choice … a choice of morals. Or you could merely turn back."*

*"There is nothing back there for me," the boy said. "I'm always pushed forward. Always. I don't know why. And I don't ever have a choice."*

*"You do now," the figure replied. "Come, sit with me. Meditate with me. You need not cross this bridge, boy. You never need to. Stay. Meditate. Be content. Bridges are for men. Not boys. Sit until you are ready."*

*"I'm ready. I'm ready to get out of here. To get back to where I belong."*

*"And where is that?" the figure asked with amusement in his tone. "How can you go to a place if you do not know your destination … or your name?"*

*The boy's eyes narrowed.*

*"Who are you?" he asked.*

*"The same as you. Nobody."*

*They stared at each other. Finally, the boy sighed.*

*"Let me go," he said. "I'm ready."*

*"Are you?"*

*"Yes."*

*The figure paused.*

*"Then remove my head from my body with your katana, boy. Do it and be on your way."*

*The boy stared at the masked man before him. A breeze ruffled their hair. After a few moments, the boy stepped forward. He raised his katana high, hesitated, then lowered it swiftly down to the man's neck-*

*He stopped.*

*"I can't," the boy said.*

*"No, you cannot," agreed the other with a knowing chuckle. "And that is why you are not ready."*

*A moment later, the robe fell inwards as though the man within had merely vanished. The boy gasped. The robe and mask lay flat before him.*

*He poked at them with his katana. There was nothing left of the man who had been speaking to him only seconds earlier. The boy stared for a moment, then knelt down and reached out. He took the mask in his hands and fingered its many buckles and straps.*

*Then he stood.*

*Just then, a stiff breeze shook the bridge. The boy had to grab the ropes to balance himself. The wind swept up the fallen robe and whisked it off the bridge and out into the open air, where it twisted and twirled. The boy watched this scene before him until the wind died, and the robe fell and disappeared from sight into the abyss below.*

*The boy stared down into the darkness for a while, and then examined the mask in his hands. He took the mask and crossed the remainder of the bridge as the sun descended below the horizon.*

# 34

"My name is Mr. Bevelaqua, although if it suits you, you can just call me Mr. B. And I will be your substitute teacher for the day."

A mummer of goodwill spread through the classroom.

Mr. Bevelaqua raised and lowered his hands to quiet them. He was a short man, pudgy and balding, with a wavy mustache.

"Okay, okay, settle down now," he said. "This isn't middle school, and this isn't recess. Mrs. Geno has left me instructions for this class, and plenty of work for you."

A girl in the front raised her hand.

"Yes?" Mr. Bevelaqua said.

"Is Mrs. Geno sick?" she asked.

"I have no information on why your teacher is not here today."

Another raised hand.

"Yes?"

"Are we going to have homework?"

Mr. Bevelaqua smiled.

"Yes, Mrs. Geno did leave me a homework assignment for you."

Groans everywhere.

"However ... however ... if this class runs smoothly—if everyone does as is expected of them—then maybe, *maybe*, I'll just happen to forget to mention that assignment to you."

This brought smiles and a few smatterings of applause. Someone whistled.

"But like I said, it's up to you," he continued. "Do your in-class work, no trouble, and we'll see."

He looked to another student whose hand was raised.

"Yes?"

"Can you be our teacher forever?"

Everyone laughed.

# 35

*It was completely dark as the boy walked through the field on the other side of the canyon. It began to slope downwards into a wide, grassy hillside. He stopped for a moment to study what was before him.*

*At the bottom of the hill began a treeline. From where he stood the boy could see the dark smudge of the forest below stretching far into the distance. He stared for a while, unconsciously fingering his katana's hilt and the black mask that was now looped to his side. He took another deep breath and began to make his way down the hillside.*

*The trees of the forest were leafless, lifeless, twisted black shapes. The boy stood at the treeline eyeing them. It wasn't until he stepped forward and touched a particular tree that he realized the trees were charred. The bark was scarred or missing, and a slight breeze brought with it the faintest scent of burn. The boy let his fingers linger on the smooth surface of the tree, and then started off into the burnt forest.*

*There were no sounds. No life. As he walked, he began to shiver slightly. It was getting cooler. Occasionally, the wind would rattle the tops of the trees like brittle bones and stir the scents of singed wood before gently dying away.*

*He walked for quite a while before he saw the light in the distance—a faint glow—and the boy made his way toward this light, cautiously, carefully, silently, and ever watchful. When he was close enough, he could see that the light was coming from a lantern that hung on one of the trees' thin branches. The flame flickered low, and was almost out.*

*He turned in a small circle, his eyes searching.*

*"Don't move," came a whispered and desperate voice.*

*The boy jumped and looked down. There, lying nearly hidden on the scarred ground, covered in what appeared to be a black sheet, were a pair of staring eyes, glistening in the light of the lantern. The boy jumped back and pulled his katana, and held it at the ready.*

*"Stay away!"*

*"Please ..." said the man's voice in a worried tone. "Keep your voice down and don't move anymore! They'll come for you! And if you move any more recklessly, you'll step into one of their traps! Now be still!"*

*The boy stared at the eyes, his own face twisted in confusion and doubt.*

*"Who are you?" the boy asked. "What—"*

*"Lower your voice!" the other warned in a hiss. "Please!"*

*The boy took a breath.*

*"Who are you?" he whispered.*

*"My name is Jimmy," the voice replied. "Jimmy Land. I said stay still! Be careful! Don't take another step!"*

*"What is this place? What are you doing here?"*

*Jimmy Land took a breath of his own.*

*"I am a scientist," he said. "A teacher. I work at the institute. Now please, you must help me out of here. You must get help."*

*"I don't even know where I am," the boy said. "And I don't know if I believe you. People—things—have been trying to kill me. I need to find a way out of all this. I—"*

*"Then we will do it together," Jimmy said. "We will—for god's sake, I said don't move!"*

*Jimmy suddenly reached out from beneath his dark covering and pointed to the boy's feet. "There is a trap at your heel! Don't move an inch!"*

*The boy looked down, behind him, and squinted, and after a moment, his eyes caught something shiny, barely poking up out of the ground.*

*He bent down.*

*"Don't touch it you imbecile!" Jimmy said.*

*The boy hesitated and turned to the man.*

*"What is it?"*

*"Like I said, it's a trap," Jimmy replied with a sigh. You touch it and you'll lose your hand for sure."*

*"Who put it there?" the boy asked.*

*"They did. The tree people."*

*The boy faced him and didn't say a word.*

*"They live here in the forest," Jimmy said. "They place traps and wait for dark and then they come and check."*

*"You have seen them? These tree people?"*

*"No, but they're here … waiting."*

*"How do you know all this?" the boy asked. "How do I know you're not trying to trick me?"*

*Jimmy pulled down his cover and revealed his leg, which was stuck in the jaws of a vicious metal trap of sharp jagged teeth.*

*"Oh," the boy gasped. "How did—"*

*"I stepped in it this morning and I've been stuck here ever since. Now please, you must help me out of it. And we must get out of here soon. We are running out of time. They'll be coming soon again."*

*"Again? You said you did not see them."*

*"I haven't. But I wasn't alone when I entered this forest this morning. I traveled in a party. And those things … they took them. Now hear boy, quick—stick your sword there into the trap and try and pry it open. Hurry!"*

*The boy eyed the man's leg.*

*"Please!"*

*The boy nodded and came forward, and carefully worked the end of his blade between the trap's jaws.*

*"Now push boy. Push!"*

*The boy pushed as hard as he could, leveraging the katana at an angle and pushing up. Jimmy muttered and cursed.*

*"No, keep going boy! Ignore me. Just get it open!"*

*The boy bit on his lower lip and added leverage to the blade once more, and again Jimmy groaned and whimpered in pain. But still, he waved the boy to continue. Finally, the metal trap began to slide open.*

*"Yes! Yes! Keep it up boy! Just a little farther!"*

*The boy added more pressure and tilted the blade farther, while Jimmy hissed and moaned. Suddenly, he slipped his foot from the jaws of the trap and pulled it away. The boy pulled out his katana and the trap snapped shut with a rattle. Jimmy held his leg and winced at the sight of it. Finally he turned to the boy.*

*"Thank you," he said. "Thank you so much. Now we must get out of here at once."*

*Jimmy tried to stand, but his leg gave way and would not hold him. He fell to a seat and cursed.*

*"Boy," he said, "I am not going to be able to walk out of here on my own and you are far too small to carry me."*

*His breathing was haggard and panicked.*

*"You must go for help. Bring someone back with you."*

*"But I don't even know where we are or where to go from here," the boy replied.*

*"Go east," Jimmy said and pointed the way. "Our camp is not but a few miles off. You won't miss it. Go and use the radio transmitter. Call for help."*

*"But I—"*

*"Please, just go. There is no more time to argue the matter!"*

*The boy stood, pondering what to do, then nodded. He sheathed his katana and started off.*

*"Wait," Jimmy said. "Take the lantern with you. You'll need it."*

*"But how will I find my way back to you?" the boy asked. "The only reason I found you before was because of it."*

*"You need it more. The tree people, they fear the light—the fire."*

*"What about you, then?"*

*"I will crawl a distance and hide. If I am lucky, they will not find me. But I'll never make it out of here if you don't bring back help. Now go. And be careful of traps—they are everywhere!"*

*The boy took the lantern from the tree and looked once more at Jimmy. He nodded, and the boy turned and ran off into the forest.*

*He had not gotten far when he heard the man scream. It was a high-pitched howl, a shriek of terror. The boy stopped and whirled in his tracks, looking back in the direction from which he had come. The scream continued for what seemed like an eternity. Then silence. The boy stared on but could see only the trees, twisted and gnarled.*

*From afar, he could see a sudden flicker of movement through the forest, barely visible. He flinched and blinked and held his breath, and held the lantern high even as his eyes squinted. But there was no sign of movement, and the boy lowered the lantern, noticing for the first time how low its flame was. He glanced back in the direction of where he had left Jimmy, then back at the flame, then at the path before him.*

*Finally, the boy began to run.*

*Suddenly, he tripped over an overgrown root and fell hard to the scorched ground, knocking his breath from him. He saw the lantern sail from his grasp and land only a few steps away. When it hit the ground, a trap snapped up around it and shattered it to pieces. Instantly, the flame was out, engulfing the boy in complete darkness.*

*There was no moon and no stars. It was as though a dark blanket had been thrown over him. He could not see his own hand a foot in front of his face.*

*When he regained his breath, he pushed himself from the ground and sat up. He rested for a moment, hearing only the beating of his heart in his ears. Soon, the silence of the forest enveloped him once more.*

*Then he heard the sound. It was a wisp of movement. The boy turned his head around, searching the darkness but seeing nothing. He held his breath. His eyes were wide, and he was gripped with fear.*

*Seconds passed.*

*Finally, something touched his eyeball, though it was so dark that the boy could not see it. He jerked away and scooted backward until he felt a tree at his back. His head turned this way and that, but again, there was nothing to be seen. And then, the tree behind him began to move, so startling the boy that the hairs on the back of his neck prickled up even as he felt his stomach sink. The tree creaked and rattled. Its branches were descending on him, covering him. The boy screamed and pulled his katana and lashed out even as the branches began to caresses his neck, his cheeks.*

*"Noo!" the boy yelled, flailing his katana until he felt the limbs sever and break away.*

*Then the tree as a whole seemed to move away. He heard it rustle and shake and thud, but it did not go far.*

*Then, more silence. The boy turned this way and that, katana out before him, cutting random strikes to the air but connecting with nothing.*

*Again, something touched his eyeball. This time, the boy not only recoiled but lashed out, and he heard the branches fall to the ground around him. He shut his eyes, clenched them tight, and lashed out again and again in a whirlwind of panic, until he finally fell to his knees. Just as he cursed, his hand touched something at his side. He began to brush it away when he realized it was only his mask.*

*He had almost forgotten about the mask.*

*He again heard the shuffle of branches nearby and the thud of movement. Instinctively, the boy pulled free the mask and pulled it over his head, pulling the straps tight and fastening the buckles as best he could in the dark.*

*He opened his eyes. And suddenly, he could see.*

*It was as though a dimmed light had been brought to the world. The boy could see the forest and the ground and his own katana. Everything was shaded in red—even the tree people, whom he could now see, too. And there were many, at least a dozen—perhaps more—completely surrounding him. They were tall, almost as tall as the trees themselves. They were hunched over low, hovering over him as closely close as possible. They were thin, like mere branches, but their general shape was of that of a human. They had stick arms and legs, resembling stilts, and even a stick head. One of the tree people was close enough for him to touch, and he could see a thin branch reaching out for his face.*

*The boy swung out with his katana and severed the finger-like branches from the arm-like limbs, and then went after the others. He lashed wildly, cutting branch from limb and limb from branch. The tree people relentlessly came toward him, trying to overtake him, but were unprepared to defend themselves against someone who could see them through the darkness. Before long, the tree people began to retreat back into the forest.*

*The boy watched them go, swiping at them threateningly with his katana, until the last one disappeared out of sight. He stood and breathed deeply, and could hear his breath through the mask echoing in his ears. Then he began walking again, this time with the shaded red light the mask provided lighting the way.*

*Before long, he could see the treeline. He quickened his pace and left the forest at a full sprint. Instantly, he could see the world again changing around him.*

*The stars appeared in the sky, and a sliver moon materialized from nowhere. But the boy did not stop. He ran until he had put a great distance between him and the forest, and only then did he reach up and unbuckle the straps and buckles around his head and removed the mask.*

# 36

Jaden sat in the back corner of the room by the windows. Outside, clouds moved in and it was growing dark. The classroom was silent. Everyone was slumped over their math books, busily writing with their pencils.

Something hit Jaden in the face. He looked down to see the folded piece of paper on the floor at his side. He looked around.

Two seats over Gloria stuck out her tongue at him and crossed her eyes at the same time.

Jaden smiled. He looked around the room, then carefully reached down and retrieved the note. He opened it.

*Do you have a girlfriend?*
*Circle*
*Yes*
*or*
*No*

Jaden suppressed a laugh, then circled "No." He refolded the paper and, after a cautionary glance, tossed it back. Gloria caught it in both hands and opened it. She smiled and wrote some more and then tossed the paper back.

*Do you have a boyfriend?*
*Circle*
*Yes*
*or*
*No*

Jaden smiled and again circled "No." Then wrote:

*I'm single.*
*Do you have Chlamydia?*
*Circle*
*Yes*

*or*
*Yes*

He tossed the note back.

Gloria opened it and laughed aloud. A few students looked up from their work. Mr. Bevelaqua looked over from the book he was reading.

Gloria quickly returned to her math book.

Jaden continued to look out the window.

# 37

*Now he could see again, even without the mask. The red hue was gone and so too the place he had just been. The boy now found himself standing on the top of a circular stone column a little more than foot or so wide. He was so startled he nearly lost his balance, his arms pin-wheeling wildly, and though he did stabilize himself after a few anxious moments sweat still streamed down his face and his heart raced.*

*He looked around. All around him was a misty open space, though through this haze he could see that the small platform on which he stood was only one of many that reached off into the distance in a vague path, like stone lily pads. They were all white, and each was as small as the one as which he now stood. Below him, the columns disappeared into a far denser mist of swirling fog.*

*The boy twisted his mouth and frowned.*

*"What now?" he muttered barely above a whisper.*

*A slight breeze lifted his hair. It was very quiet.*

*The boy jumped from his column to the next. He made the jump with ease, but almost lost his balance again when he landed. He stretched his arms out and bent over, steadying himself. Then he stood tall, took a deep breath, and jumped again. This time he landed on the top of the next column with better care and balance. He paused a moment and then jumped to the next. He looked over his shoulder to take in his progress. The columns were close and he had not gone far at all.*

*The boy faced forward. Again his mouth twisted. He jumped to the next column.*

*It was some time before the boy came upon the black column. It was so dark and in such contrast to the others that the boy stopped to stare at it for a moment. It was stone, too, but its surface was different from the rest. It was chipped and worn, and protruding from its midsection was a piece of metal, shaped like an upside-down "u," rusted and old. Attached to this piece of metal was a chain that dangled over the side and stretched down into the mist.*

*The boy jumped a column closer and squinted his eyes to investigate.*

*He unsheathed his katana and squatted down at the knees. He reached out with his blade and poked the chain with its tip. The chain was very thick and hung heavy. Its links were big enough to squeeze his head through. It did not move. He stood and resheathed his katana, then jumped onto the black column and squatted down again. He touched the piece of metal and then the chain itself. Both were cold. The boy looked back over his shoulder, then ahead at the columns still to come. There seemed to be little difference in them.*

*The boy let out a huff of air and took hold of the chain. After straddling the column with his legs, he began to lower himself down into the mist. Slowly, the mist enveloped him and within seconds, he could see nothing but the white before his eyes. He could no longer see the chain in his hands or the dark column. But he continued on, down and down, for a long time. He did not stop. He just continued down, one chain link at a time, one breath at a time.*

*One link. One breath.*

*The boy held his breath for a beat. He could now see something through the mist below. He paused, his hands clamped tightly around the chain, and stared below into darkness. He took a breath and continued down. Soon, he was through the mist, and the column came to an abrupt end at the edge of the mist, as though it dared go no farther. The chain, however, continued downward.*

*Below was nothing but darkness.*

*Suddenly, the boy saw a single flicker of light, which seemed far away. But he knew he had seen it, so he let his legs go off the column and twirled them instead around the chain, which did not sway even an inch under his weight. He began to make his way down through the darkness, toward the light. As he continued to descend, the light below never seemed to grow any closer. Before long, the boy's arms were tiring, aching, and his fingers had long gone numb.*

*Just when it seemed as though he could not go any farther, he saw that the light appeared closer. He gathered himself and found renewed energy, and continued his descent.*

*Finally, he reached the light. It was a simple bulb that hung from the chain and the boy paused a moment before trying to climb past it. His legs suddenly dangled down into open space—the chain had abruptly ended. He clutched the chain in his hands as tight as he could.*

*He looked down and was surprised to see that the ground was only a little more than a body's-length below. He lowered himself to the chain's last link and hung with his arms above his head, and then let go. He dropped with a thud, and looked up.*

*The light bulb illuminated a small area around him. He stood and looked around. He was standing in a small circle of light, and the ground at his feet was actually a wooden floor. It creaked slightly with his weight. There was nothing in the circle of light, and he could see nothing beyond its edges but darkness.*

*There was no sound. The boy listened, cocking his head just so.*

*Thump. Thump.*

*He heard it coming from a distance beyond the circle of light, coming from the darkness.*

*Thump. Thump.*

*And then a figure stepped from the darkness and into the circle of light.*

*The boy stepped back, afraid.*

*Before him stood a massive figure that towered over him, a huge, muscular figure. The figure wore taxed and tight spandex of black and blood-red, and a skin-squeezing mask of gold with a silver lightning bolt on the forehead.*

*The masked man stepped forward, his gleaming golden boots laced high up the leg.*

*Thump. Thump.*

*"You challenge me?" came a booming voice from behind the slit in the mask. It was a question brimming with indignity.*

*"N-no," the boy replied, barely above a whisper. "I-I didn't."*

*"You did! You entered the arena!"*

*"I didn't know—I-I don't want to bother you. I—"*

*"Silence! You have stepped foot on holy ground and now you must pay!"*

*"But I didn't mean anything. I just want to go. I just want—"*

*"You will go! Broken in half!"*

*"Please …"*

*The boy backed to the very edge of light, his hand instinctively at his katana's hilt.*

*"Just let me go. Let me leave," he pleaded.*

*The massive masked man stared back at him, opening and clinching his fists.*

*The boy pulled his katana and held it before him.*

*"Stay back!"*

*The masked man froze.*

*"You bring a weapon into the arena?" he asked. "This is forbidden! You are coward! You are weak!"*

*"How do I get out of here?" the boy asked. "Just tell me and I'll go."*

*The man's massive chest rose and fell with heavy breaths. His fists curled tight. Knuckles popped and cracked. Veins began to pulse in his thick arms and even thicker neck.*

*"How dare you?!"*

*As the masked man began to move forward, the boy lashed out with his blade and caught the masked man around the hip with a deep cut. The katana became embedded—stuck.*

*The masked man looked down at the wound and the katana end that stuck into his flesh, then lifted his gaze to the boy. His eyes were now red with hatred.*

*"I—" the boy began.*

*But it was too late. The masked man reached down and grabbed the boy by the neck and with one upward pull, thrust him up and over his head, crashing to the ground behind him like a doll. Then the masked man reached down and pulled the katana from his hip and flung it hard to the ground, where it stuck upright with a clang.*

*He whirled around. The boy had just managed to raise his head and shake it when the masked man kicked him hard in the stomach. The boy gasped a scream and was again lifted off the ground and sent crashing back down in another helpless heap.*

*"You will suffer! You will beg! You will cry!" the masked man shouted.*

*Thump. Thump. Thump.*

*The masked man strode forward, grabbed the boy by the back of his hakima pants, pulled him up, and threw him high into the air again. The boy sailed up and up, twirling, and his head smashed hard into something.*

*There was a pop.*

*There was a small explosion of glass as the light bulb smashed against his head, and everything had gone dark. The boy began his fall, but it stopped abruptly when his leg became entangled in something. The sudden jerk on his leg sent waves of pain through his body. He was caught up in the chain—his foot wedged between links—and he dangled upside-down, his hakima pants falling all the way up past his knees to his thighs.*

*All was black.*

*Thump. Thump. Thump. Thump. Thump.*

*"Where are you, you little coward?!" the masked man yelled. "Where are you?!"*

*He could hear the man moving below, searching. His voice was not far away. Slowly, the boy reached up for the chain and pulled himself upright. He paused for breath, then yanked his foot free with a searing pain, wincing and biting his lips. But he did not make a sound.*

*Thump. Thump. Thump.*

*"You cannot hide forever!" the masked man shouted.*

*The boy hung above, clutching the chain. He might have stayed that way forever, but a thought struck him—a thought and a memory.*

*The masked man stomped about, reaching this way and that, kicking the air. He cursed and growled and clenched his fists, over and over again, and now stood directly below the chain. Suddenly, the boy in the mask dropped down on top of him, swinging his sandaled feet and letting out a vicious battle cry. He plowed into the masked man's face with a crunch and a pop.*

*The masked man staggered backward and fell to a knee, holding his face with his hands. The boy landed in a soft crouch a short distance away, and stood. He watched the masked man in the red hue of the mask.*

*"You …" the masked man breathed with venom. "How dare you?!"*

*He stood and lowered his hands from his face. Blood seeped from his mouth and down his pulsing neck. His chest heaved.*

*"The darkness will not save you, boy!"*

*Thump. Thump.*

*"I can hear you breathing! I will find you! I will break you!"*

*The boy held his breath, stood motionless, and watched as the massive masked man stalked forward through the darkness—arms out, hands open, groping and seeking. Just beyond the masked man, the boy could see his katana sticking up from the ground, waiting for him.*

*He took a single step to the side, and the masked man turned his head in the boy's direction. He paused, then charged forward.*

*Thump. Thump. Thump.*

*The boy dove between his legs at a roll and came up next to the katana. He grabbed the hilt and pulled, but it was stuck in the floor. The masked man whirled in his direction, his head cocked. And the boy tugged on the katana with all his might.*

*"There you are!"*

*Thump. Thump.*

*"There you are!"*

*The masked man came forward yelling, and the boy yelled too. His muscles tensed, and he managed to pull the katana free.*

*The punch hit the boy in the shoulder and sent him tumbling to the ground. The katana spun away.*

*"Ha!" the masked man yelled triumphantly, and continued to come at him, reaching low to the ground, feeling for the boy. The boy lay face-down nearby and stayed there as the masked man's fingers slipped passed him, just inches away.*

*"Where did you go?"*

*Again, the masked man's fingers came close, but the boy remained frozen. He waited until the masked man turned his search in another direction.*

*He saw his katana then, right there at his side. He grabbed it and curled his fingers around its hilt. Some of his knuckles were bleeding. He gathered himself and got to his feet, swaying.*

*"I'm here," the boy said tiredly, with a hard swallow. "Come and get me."*

*The masked man turned.*

*"Say it. Say it one more time, boy!" he dared.*

*Thump.*

*"I ..."*

*Thump.*

*"... am ..."*

*Thump. Thump.*

*"... right ..."*

*Thump. Thump. Thump.*

*"... here."*

*The masked man grasped outward as though trying to smother the boy in a hug. Instead, the katana sliced into his chest and for a moment, neither boy nor man moved. Then the boy drew back his blade and the masked man fell to his knees clutching himself.*

*"You ..."*

*The boy faced the masked man before him.*

*"I just want to go."*

*Then the boy cut out and severed the masked man's head from his body. Blood sprayed, splattering the boy's mask and clothes. But he did not move. He stayed until the blood had stopped and the body had sagged into a motionless heap. Only then did the ronin boy turn and walk away into the darkness.*

# 38

"Don't you think Mr. B looked an awful lot like that guy the Pink Panther was always pestering in them cartoons?" Gloria asked.

Jaden smiled. "Maybe a little."

"More than a little … you see that mustache? Come on."

They both laughed.

"So," Gloria said, "how *was* that vacation?"

"Fine."

They walked slowly down the hall together as other students rushed past them to get to their next classes.

"You know, if you're going to miss Monday through Thursday you might as well take Friday off, too."

"I considered it."

"Yeah, I can tell. You look pretty miserable to be here," she said.

"I'm just tired I think."

"Well, maybe if you went to bed a little earlier and stopped staying up all night watching bad movies on the phone with me …"

"I'll see what I can do about that."

They walked together for a few moments.

"You haven't lately."

"Haven't?"

"Watched bad movies with me."

"I'm sorry."

"I called a few times, but your mother said you were sleeping. Were you?"

"I guess."

Gloria looked at Jaden for a moment.

"I skipped once because of a skunk. Did I ever tell you that?"

"No, I think I'd have remembered that. A skunk?"

"I kid you not. See, late this night, this skunk apparently decided it'd be sooo cool to camp outside my bedroom window and he must have sprayed or something, 'cause the smell made me nauseous. I couldn't get any sleep. I mean literally, none. And so there I was at six in the morning with these bloodshot eyes … there was no way I could make it."

Jaden laughed.

"Laugh it up, but I'll tell you, that thing stunk," Gloria said.

"Skipping school because of a skunk," Jaden said with a chuckle. "That's a first. Is that what your note said?"

"My note said I had massive diarrhea. Like projectile diarrhea."

They both laughed.

"But no, seriously, that skunk kept me up all night."

"You're crazy," Jaden said.

"Crazy? Have you ever smelled a skunk's butt before? Well, it ain't no treat, I can tell you that."

They came to a T in the hall.

"I'll see you at lunch," Gloria said and waved.

Jaden turned down another hall, alone.

# 39

*This time, the darkness, even with the vision provided by the mask, was too dark, too dense, to see through. The boy walked on before the darkness began to give way to shadows, and as these shadows lengthened, shapes began to form.*

*At first, they were very indistinct, but soon he could make out shapes. By the time the darkness had faded altogether, he realized his surroundings had changed yet again. He was no longer surprised.*

*He only sighed and stopped.*

*Now he was standing in an orchard of apple trees. The sky was gloomy and the air was wet. The grass at his feet was soggy, as though it had just rained. A fog drifted lazily through the rows of apple trees. The boy sucked on his bottom lip and instinctively touched his hilt.*

*He took off his mask and looped it to his side, and took another deep breath.*

*He looked at the ground and saw many apples lying about. Some were ripe for eating, though most were small, shriveled, and brown. He stepped on one and it mashed beneath his sandal. He brushed the hair from his eyes and pulled a ripe one off a tree and bit into it.*

*It was good—quite good, in fact. He devoured two more before he continued slowly along the row. The row stretched on uneventfully until there came a slight rise. The boy climbed the rise and stopped at its peak.*

*Below him was a clearing, and at its center was a single massive tree. But this tree had oranges on it. Its contrast to the rows of apple trees was striking. The boy made his way down into the clearing and stopped in front of the tree. It was indeed massive, and as he looked up into it, he could see hundreds and hundreds of large oranges, hanging just out of reach, taunting him. His mouth began to water and even though his stomach was full of apples, the sight of the oranges caused it to rumble.*

*He wanted some oranges.*

*He scanned the ground and was surprised to see that not a single orange lay there. He stepped forward and looked up again, twisting his mouth and walking around the trunk, pondering how to reach the fruit. The trunk was wide, and as the boy stepped around it he looked for holes, grooves, knots—anything he could use to climb. But there were none.*

*The bark was smooth, almost unnaturally so. He touched the tree and when he pulled his hand back, his fingertips were stained brown. His forehead furrowed.*

*"Who?" came a voice.*

*The startled boy jumped and pulled out his katana.*

*"Who?" the voice asked again.*

*The boy looked up into the tree with narrowed eyes. There was some rustling, and an owl poked its head down through the leaves.*

*"Hoo?"*

*The boy let out a heavy, relieved sigh and resheathed his weapon.*

*"You almost got yourself into trouble, little fella," the boy said with a chuckle.*

*"Hoo?" the owl answered back.*

*"Care to throw me down a couple oranges, friend?"*

*The owl twisted its head, as though wondering if it should, then turned back to him.*

*"Didn't think so."*

*The boy lowered his head and eyed the trunk again.*

*"Hoo? Hoo? Who are you?"*

*The boy looked up.*

*"What? What did you—"*

*"Who are you?" the owl said again, and blinked twice.*

*"I-I … you can speak?!"*

*Two blinks.*

*"Who?"*

*The boy hesitated.*

*"I don't know … who are you?" he asked.*

*The owl blinked, paused, and then blinked again. Then it pulled its head back up into the cover of leaves and was gone.*

*"Wait!" the boy called out. "You can talk? You understand me? Come back! Hey, please come back!"*

*But the owl did not come back and the boy stared up into the tree for a long time before he lowered his head. His neck now hurt and he rubbed it.*

*Just then, something hit him in the head. It was an orange. The boy snatched it up and held it in his hands smiling. Then he looked up into the tree again.*

*"Thank you, friend."*

*But there was no reply.*

*The boy eagerly began to peel the orange and had gotten around halfway through when the fuzzy orange-and-white ball inside suddenly blinked.*

*He gasped and dropped the orange to the ground. It rolled a few feet and then came to a rest facing him. It was an eye. Watching him.*

*It blinked again.*

*A shiver whipped through the boy's body and stiffened the hairs on his arms and neck. He looked at the half-peeled eyeball in shocked disgust.*

*"Who?" came the voice from above.*

*The boy looked up.*

*The hundreds of oranges had all split open. And now hundreds of eyes watched the boy.*

*The boy's mouth fell open, and he stepped backward.*

*In unison, every eye blinked.*

*"Who?" said the voice.*

*But it was not coming from above—it was much closer.*

*The boy looked down and saw the owl standing just a few steps away, watching him intently. It twisted its head around and blinked twice.*

*"Who?" it asked again.*

*Then it ducked its head and poked at the orange on the ground, sticking its pointy beak deep into the eye, and began feeding. The eye began to bleed out.*

*The owl lifted its head, its beak dripping with blood and flesh.*

*"Who?"*

*The boy turned and ran.*

*Rain began to fall, steady and cold.*

*The boy ran through the apple orchard, running and never looking back. Soon, the orchard was gone, far out of sight behind him, but he ran on, barely seeing any of what lay before him. The rain was blinding now, and the ground was becoming muddy. He slipped but did not fall, and ran on still until finally, this ronin boy stopped and dropped to his knees.*

*He could run no farther. He bowed his head as the rain continued to fall.*

# 40

"Five minutes of journal time," Mrs. Sharon said as she stood in front of the class.

The desks before her were situated in the shape of a giant "u," and she stood at its center.

"And remember, if you can't find anything to write about on your own, if those creative juices are a little sapped, then choose from the Narrative Starters on the board," she said, pointing to the blackboard behind her. "Remember, free-flow, let the words come. Nothing is taboo."

Jaden stared at the blank piece of paper before him. His mouth twisted. He looked up at the board and read the Narrative Starters.

> *In front of him was a big board with three flashing buttons: red, yellow, and blue. Which was the right one?*
>
> *A tiny voice asked: Is he the one?*
>
> *Think about what success means to you. Do you measure it in financial terms, in terms of human relationships, or by other criteria? Explain your definition of success.*
>
> *All I want for Christmas ...*
>
> *Relate to your report card.*
>
> *Compare and contrast a "nobody" and a "somebody."*
>
> *Argue whether life is a line or a circle.*
>
> *Write a new poem.*
>
> *What do you envision schools of the future to be like? Will they be larger, smaller, or more computerized than today? Consider what a class would be like at SRH in fifty years.*

Jaden frowned, and then began to write:

*The tree was big, huge really, with all these wide branches and this thick trunk. So it was strange (I've always thought so, anyway) that it could have just fallen over without anyone hearing it. But maybe it was just all the wind that night that covered it's toppling to the ground.*

*It was (as in a cartoon) split seemingly right down the middle and the smell of burnt wood lingered long after. The wood was black toward the center. And splintery.*

*I remember looking at it—this tree—it had fallen through our back fence and into our backyard and the snow had begun to cover it, and it slumped there like some kind of fallen man or something. Maybe even a corpse. And I remember thinking it was sad at first. But then the more I stared, the less sad I felt, like I just knew somehow that the tree was meant to fall, to die, and it was happier now. I was alone and it was night and I stared at it for a long, long time. At some point I looked up into the sky and let the falling snow touch my face. I shivered some. I think I may have smiled some too. Maybe. I was only four years old. It was my first-ever memory.*

Jaden looked down at what he had written. Then he crumpled it up and brushed it aside.

# 41

*Through the patter of raindrops, the boy could hear a sound. It was soft and distant, but coming closer. Finally, he saw a covered wagon roll into view.*

*The horse pulling the wagon was slight and dark, its hoofs smacking the wet earth. It came close and slowed. The wagon's large wooden wheels creaked and stopped. A door swung open in the back of the wagon, and warm, inviting light spilled out.*

*"Join me," a woman's voice said from inside the wagon.*

*The boy did not stir.*

*"Please."*

*The boy stood and walked to the open door and peered inside. The interior was colored in shades of red and brown, and he could see a little kettle on a raised burner.*

*"Please," repeated the voice. "It is wet and cold. Come warm up."*

*He hesitated, but finally stepped up into the wagon and pulled the door shut behind him. The inside of the wagon was covered in cushions and pillows. It was snug and tight, yet comforting. A single lantern bathed its interior in a delicate light. There was a woman sitting at the far end. She appeared old, but not too old. Perhaps her elaborate dress hid a few years away, as did her makeup and flowing dark hair.*

*She smiled.*

*"Sit," she said. "Do not worry about the pillows. They will dry."*

*The boy took in his surroundings and sat on a large fluffy pillow that engulfed him like a puffy cloud.*

*They stared at one another for a moment.*

*"Are you hungry?" the woman asked. "You must be. You may have some soup, if you would like."*

*The boy eyed the woman cautiously, then nodded and came forward.*

*"There are bowls and a spoon to the side."*

*The boy took a bowl and scooped out what he could.*

*"It is hot mind you," the woman warned.*

*But the boy had already swallowed eagerly. The woman did not speak until he was done.*

*"You may have another if you—"*

*The boy nodded before she could even finish, and was already scooping more into his bowl. The woman smiled as he finished off another serving, and another after that. The boy finally lowered the spoon and placed the bowl back where he had found it.*

*"Good?" the woman asked, as the wagon begun to move forward again.*

*"Very," the boy replied. "Thank you."*

*The woman nodded.*

*"Who are you?" the boy finally asked.*

*The woman sighed.*

*"Always the first question," she said, "and always the least important."*

*She paused.*

*"I am merely an old woman. That is all."*

*For a few moments, the only sound was the rain pattering on the ceiling above them.*

*"Like the light of a falling star," the woman abruptly sang in a near whisper. She smiled again, then continued.*

*pray his light travels far.*
*Pray it sparkles through the dark*
*pray much light his falling spark.*
*Give the light of a star*
*a tiny light, it travel far.*
*Little light glow the dark*
*do it just, his falling spark.*
*Time is night where stars do fall*
*perhaps black holes, no light at all.*
*Light the way, he wish to be*
*when he reach eternity.*
*Little lights glow the dark*
*even just a falling spark.*
*Such a spark, say goodbye*
*say hello, tear his eye.*
*Such tiny light, barely see*
*through the fogs, wind blow free.*
*Sleet and hail pierce his face*
*his little light they will erase.*
*What he did, what he said*
*will it shine his body dead.*

*A long moment passed.*

*"Where am I?" the boy asked in barely more than a whisper.*

*Again the woman's lips curved into a smile.*

*"Not 'where,'" the woman said, "but 'who.'"*

*"Then who?" asked the boy in an even softer voice than before.*

*"The fates guide you," she replied. "They guide you even now. Like the winds, they gently push you along. Turning you in directions, leading you—leading you to those like me."*

*"And what are you?"*

*"But I wonder why. Where do you go from here? Where does it lead you next?"*

*"I do not understand any of this."*

*"No one sees the end until it is upon them."*

*"Please," the boy said. "I'm lost. And things don't make sense. And everywhere I go people—things—are trying to hurt me."*

*The wagon abruptly stopped. The horse whinnied above the rain.*

*"They come now," said the woman.*

*Just then, the door at the back of the wagon opened to the darkness outside.*

*"Who?" the boy asked.*

*The woman didn't answer. The boy went to the door and looked out. They had stopped at the bottom of a rather steep hill. The rain had intensified, and muddy rivers flowed down the hill around them. At the top of the hill, he could see two shadowy figures: one tall, one short.*

*The two figures slowly made their way down the road, side by side, their matching dark cloaks hiding their faces like living shadows. When they had come to within a few paces of the wagon, they stopped. They stood motionless, staring straight ahead into the wagon. Finally, the taller of the two stepped forward.*

*"How long has it been, old woman?" asked a man's voice from beneath the hood.*

*"Why have you come?" the old woman asked.*

*No response.*

*"I have nothing to offer you," she said.*

*The tall figure laughed.*

*"But we have traveled so far to find you," he said in a mocking tone. "You are not a gracious host."*

*"And you are not a welcome guest," she shot back.*

*There was a still, tense moment that lingered between them, and then the tall man reached up and pulled back his hood, revealing the dark-skinned, sunken face of an old man. His long black hair was pulled tight into many small cornrows, and his eyes were bright white—empty and blind.*

*"Not a welcome guest?" he said with a wry smile, as he turned in the direction of the boy.*

*"Please leave," the woman said.*

*"And if we do not? What then? What will you do?"*

*The woman said nothing.*

*"Perhaps you would try and kill me if I do not leave?" the man said. "Perhaps like before? You think it, of that I have no doubt."*

*The old man put his hand on his companion's shoulder.*

*"But I ask, would you be so bold, so eager, to try the same," he said, pulling back his companion's hood, "to a child?"*

*The woman's face quivered slightly as she saw the small girl. The girl was young, perhaps younger than the boy. Her face was white and beautiful, her black hair knotted tight into two points at the top of her head, resembling two horns.*

*"Her name is Tko," the old man said with a grin. "She is my newest champion. And I assure you, old woman, you will have to kill her before you kill me."*

*Tko stepped in front of the old man. He gently placed his hands on her shoulders. Tko brushed back her cloak and clutched the hilt of her now visible katana.*

*It was pink and shinny.*

*"As you well know, my fighting days are far behind me," the old woman said. "That is why I have chosen my own new champion."*

*She turned an upraised palm to the boy.*

*The boy stared at her for a moment, his eyes widened with disbelief.*

*"What? Me?" he said.*

*The old woman nodded.*

*"Your coming was no coincidence," she said.*

*"But … but," he sputtered, shaking his head. "I don't think you understand. I'm not supposed to be here. I'm not apart of any of this. I-I don't even know how to fight. Not really."*

*The old woman smiled at him, and her eyes fell to his side, to his katana.*

*"The smell and stain of blood upon your steel says otherwise," she said.*

*The boy's mouth fell open. He began to speak, but the old man spoke first.*

*"Shall we be done with the dramatics?" the man said. "It is wet. And me and my champion have a long walk ahead of us."*

*"Very well," the old woman said, then turned to the boy. "Leave the door open so that I might hear. And don't be long. I've put the water on for tea."*

*The boy looked at the woman, then at the two outside waiting. Then he turned back to the woman.*

*"Go along," she said, shooing him away with a few flicks of her wrist, "I'll be waiting."*

*The boy stared at her for another moment, then stepped to the open door.*

*"Listen, I don't know who you are or what any of this is about but ..." the boy said.*

*The old man muttered something to his champion and stepped back. As he did, Tko quickly unsheathed her katana and lunged for the boy.*

*He had only a split second to react, and dove out of the open doorway to the ground outside just in time. He landed hard in the mud and had just begun to stand when Tko swung at him again. She aimed high, for his head, and as he ducked away, he could feel the blade slice through his hair.*

*"Hey!" the boy yelled, pulling his own katana free. "Wait a second! Stop!"*

*But the little girl would not hear him. She came again quickly, and this time had he not had his own blade out, it would have been his end. He managed to parry her strike away.*

*Tko glared and bared her teeth, and circled like a hungry animal.*

*"You're just a little girl. I don't want to—"*

*Tko slashed out for his midsection and cut his clothing as he jumped back.*

*The rain continued to pelt them in torrents.*

*Tko again charged in. The boy rolled away and came to his feet, his katana at the ready.*

*"Make her stop!" he yelled at the old man. "This is crazy! I don't want to hurt her!"*

*Tko came again, cutting a wide arc. The boy lunged aside, but she managed to catch him along the shoulder, drawling blood. The boy yelled out in pain and whirled on the girl with sudden anger in his eyes. She came forward, swinging low. He jumped to avoid her blade and struck her with the hilt of his katana in the nose. Her head rocked back as blood sprayed from her nostrils. She dropped her katana and fell to her knees, her hands holding her broken nose. Blood seeped through her fingers.*

*"Up Tko! Finish him!" the old man shouted.*

*"No! Enough!" the boy yelled.*

*"Tko! Now!"*

*Tko stood and picked up her katana. She lowered her other hand from her face and gripped the blade with both hands, blood still flowing from her nostrils. She faced the boy with swollen yet determined eyes and stepped forward.*

*The boy waited, his katana at the ready.*

*"Don't!" he warned.*

*Tko raised her katana high. The boy raised his blade, too.*

*They attacked, and passed by each other exchanging positions.*

*They faced each other. A long moment passed. Then Tko dropped her weapon and fell forward to the muddy ground and did not move.*

*The old man stared at the fallen body before him, then stepped forward and leaned down. He took the katana in his hand and stood. Then he faced the boy.*

*"Beautiful," the old man said in awe, as he resheathed the katana at his own side.*

*Then he turned and without another word began to make his way back up the hill.*

*The boy watched the old man walk away, then he resheathed his own katana and went to the girl, who lay face-down in the mud. He knelt and turned her over onto her back. Her eyes were open, frozen in a look of surprise. The boy looked into her dead eyes, then stood and went back to the wagon. He violently threw open the door, nearly tearing it from its hinges.*

*"What was that?!" he yelled as he climbed inside, whipping the wet hair from his face.*

*He noticed that the interior of the wagon had changed. It was no longer draped in lavish cloth and pillow, and the burner with the boiling tea was gone.*

*So was almost everything else. The wagon was empty.*

*The old woman was gone, too. Only a single lantern remained hanging from a hook in the ceiling, whose flame was nearly extinguished. The boy clenched his fists in anger, and turned to leave.*

*Just then, something caught his eye: an object glowing green from the far side. The boy's eyes narrowed as he strode forward. The object was a small vial of green liquid. He bent down and picked it up, twirling it in his fingers as he studied it.*

*Puzzled, he shook the vial. Then he stood.*

*He shook his head and shoved the vial of green liquid into his hakima pants pocket. He turned and saw that the door had closed again. He eyed the closed door as though it were an obstacle—an enemy.*

*Rain continued to pelt the outside of the wagon.*

*The boy stepped forward and kicked the door open …*

# 42

"Before we begin, Jaden, you are the only person who has yet to read aloud their Robert Frost poem parody," Mrs. Sharon said. "The rest of the class finished up earlier this week, but you were absent."

She held out the paper.

"Would you? It's already graded, but everyone else had to read theirs, so …"

Jaden hesitated.

"You don't have to stand in front of the class," she said. "Your seat will do."

Mrs. Sharon placed the paper before him. He looked down at the grade, then at Mrs. Sharon. She smiled and winked. Jaden licked his lips and cleared his throat. All the other students were waiting. He coughed, then began in a low voice:

"Whose webs these are I think I know.
The swirly pattern as it goes.
Might it see me stop and stare,
To watch it spin and dance on air.

My little friend must think it queer
I stand so close and am so near.
Between the shelf and ceiling high,
It hides in darkness from my eyes.

The string of silk begins to shake
Its creator returns, there's no mistake
And the only sounds are the sweep,
Of my backing up uncertain feet.

The web is lovely, but dark and deep
Are the eyes the creator keeps
And another dance before it sleeps
And another dance before it sleeps."

Jaden looked down at the paper in silence.

"Very good," Mrs. Sharon said, beginning to clap, and the class clapped with her, unenthusiastically.

Then Mrs. Sharon turned back to the board and began to talk about *The Great Gatsby.*

# 43

*… and was greeted by a world of lush, dense green. Big leafy plants and wide bending trees were everywhere. Moss grew low and high, and vines draped and circled around in wild loops. Wild flowers and wild grass was abundant, and the sounds of birds and other animals and insects echoed. There was a living buzz, and all was wet and dewy.*

*The boy looked over his shoulder and saw that he was no longer standing in the doorway of the covered wagon, but instead in the opening of a small cave. It was dark inside, but he could see well enough to make out a slight alcove. The cave was not too deep.*

*The boy turned back to the outside and took in his new surroundings. He was standing on a rocky outcropping on the side of a small hill. If he had taken another step forward, he would have fallen.*

*Spread out before him was a jungle. He took a deep breath and carefully began to make his way down the hill to the jungle floor. At the bottom, he looked back up and could no longer see the alcove or the cliff he had just stood on—all was hidden by the deep, dense jungle.*

*The ronin boy began to pick his way through the trees and bush and vine, stepping over slippery rocks, hidden holes, and fallen trees, until he reached a clearing on the jungle floor. He stopped and rested on a stump. He could hear the sounds of creeping movement nearby.*

*The boy's eyes narrowed as he looked around suspiciously. There was silence for a moment, but then the familiar sounds returned. The boy stood.*

*"Who is there?" he called out.*

*There came no reply. Now accustomed to such circumstances, the boy did not waste any time in pulling out his katana.*

*"I said who's there?"*

*His question was again answered only with silence. This time, however, the silence was deafening: no birds, no insects, no sounds at all. Only complete, unnerving silence.*

*"I have fought many and much to be in this place, and I will not back down now," he called out. "I am not afraid."*

*But his voice betrayed him. Suddenly, almost as though sensing his fear, the source of the menacing sound slipped from the treeline and came into view.*

*It was a tiger. For a moment, the boy stood frozen, staring at the beast, which stared back at him. The boy's eyes glazed and his temples pounded rhythmically with his heart.*

*"... gods ..." The boy breathed, unaware that he had spoken.*

*The tiger's coat was shaded in black and orange and white, and its eyes were as green as jade. It was twice the size of any tiger the boy had ever seen, or hoped to see. Its paws were as big as frying pans, its whiskers looked as long as the boy's arms, and its head was impossibly large.*

*Unconsciously, the boy had already taken two steps backward—his katana forgotten in his hand. The tiger watched the boy retreat, its eyes gleaming.*

*The boy nearly tripped over a twisted root, but did not take his eyes from the beast before him. He took another step back, then another. He quickly realized he had reached the far side of the clearing, with the underbrush at his back.*

*The tiger stared. The boy stared. Seconds passed.*

*Then the boy turned and dove wildly into the jungle.*

*The tiger watched the boy go. It waited for a beat or two, then gave chase.*

*Leaves, branches, and other wild growth whipped the boy's face as he sprinted frantically through the jungle. He could hear the tiger pursuing him. It did not sound far off, and he could tell it was closing fast. The boy brushed away a vine and became tangled for just a second. His heart pounded, and he could almost feel the beast upon him, its breath now audible. All hairs on the boy's neck went rigid, and he knew it was the end.*

*He turned and saw the tiger racing toward him, its oversized head slipping open revealing its many enormous, glistening teeth.*

*The tiger lunged.*

*The boy screamed.*

*Instantly, the boy could feel himself falling away. First went his footing, and he found himself on his back and sliding away as the beast dove over and past him. The boy did not stop, though. He continued his slide, trying desperately to reach out and stop his descent. But he could not. The walls of this forest slide were wet with the rain and slick with decaying leaves.*

*He slid on, the world whizzing past him in a blur of green. In the distance, he heard the tiger roar with rage, and his backward slide continued. Suddenly, he felt the ground beneath him disappear.*

*He was falling now. Falling away from the jungle and out into open space. He could see the bright blue sky above him. For a moment, he felt peace, comfort, and relief. But then his body turned and he could see what awaited him below.*

*He braced himself as he plunged into the dark awaiting water.*

# 44

"It's Friday," Mr. Garret reminded. "I assume everyone knows what they are doing, so unless there are any questions, I'll be in my office. Remember to sign yourself in before you leave."

Mr. Garret glanced at a student or two, then walked into his office and shut the door, leaving it slightly ajar.

Students immediately began moving about, talking in groups of two's or three's, showing each other their pictures, adjusting cameras, and loading film.

Jaden settled himself in a back booth and sat down with a huff. He closed his eyes and rested for a moment.

"So where have you been?" Clarence asked.

"Home," Jaden replied without opening his eyes.

"Sick?"

"No."

"Why then?"

"Because."

"Because why?"

"Just because. You've got something to show me?"

"Oh yeah," Clarence said. "You all right?"

"Huh?" Jaden said, opening his eyes.

"You look … I don't know … distracted or something."

Jaden paused.

"Small headache," he muttered.

"Need aspirin?" Clarence asked as he unzipped his bag.

"No, I'm fine."

"You sure? I've got plenty. It won't—"

"I'm sure."

Clarence twisted his mouth and lowered his bag.

"So what's the big surprise?" Jaden asked.

"Come into the dark room," Clarence said. "You're absolutely not gonna believe this."

Jaden got up and followed Clarence.

# 45

*The water was murky and gloomy, dark and thick, warm like melted chocolate, or blood. When the boy resurfaced, he was surprised to find that his skin was not covered in a slimy layer of something.*

*He brushed the wet hair from his eyes and looked around. He was treading water in a shadowed, small, almost circular body of water that was sheltered by a wide lip of natural rock. Above him was a canopy of willow trees that block out most of the sunlight and sky.*

*Gone was the jungle. Gone was the beast.*

*It was quiet here. He could hear the water dripping off him.*

*The boy swam to the edge of the water and rested. Once he caught his breath, he felt the rock on the edge of the pool with his fingers. It was smooth, and a few spots were much lighter than the rest, and seemed to glow in contrast.*

*He stayed there for a while. The warm water of the pool was soothing and relaxing. He was exhausted, and part of him wanted to slip back into the water and just float, or even sink. Anything to avoid moving.*

*His closing eyelids opened wider at the sight of a spark or firefly—something that flashed before his field of vision and then disappeared. He blinked and opened his eyes wide. He was now wide awake again. The idea of falling asleep in this strange place seemed absurd and foolish, and he shook his head and rubbed at his eyes to regain his alertness. He reached his arms over the lip of the pool to pull himself out, but stopped when he heard giggles.*

*They were soft giggles, but seemed to be coming from nearby. The boy looked around, but could not see anyone.*

*More giggles.*

*"I am not afraid anymore," he called out, still looking around for the source of laughter.*

*The giggles stopped and a few of the leaves rustled. His hand fell to his katana's hilt.*

*"You're a cutesey-wootsey!" came a faint voice from nearby.*

*The boy saw a light flash through the leaves and then disappear. More giggles followed.*

*"He's a hugsey-wugsey!"*

*"A pinchey-winchey!"*

*"A lovey-dubey!"*

*Giggles and giggles.*

*"Who are you?" the boy asked. "What are you?"*

*Silence.*

*Suddenly, a glowing blue light dipped down below the leaves.*

*"My names Tibby!" came a squeaky faint voice from the floating thing. It had wings and a body.*

*"A fairy," the boy muttered to himself.*

*There were more giggles as three more dropped from above.*

*"I'm Libby!"*

*"I'm Vibby!"*

*"My name's Gibby!" said the last, who curtsied with a twirl.*

*The four fairies darted about, their blue light leaving behind a partial trail, and then they came to a stop side by side, looking down upon the boy.*

*For a moment, the boy could do little more than stare, his mouth agape. This made the fairies giggle with bashful glee as they all covered their mouths and blushed.*

*Finally the boy said, "Where are we? What is this place?"*

*More giggles.*

*"Oh silly! You know where!" said Tibby.*

*"But I don't," the boy replied. "I am lost."*

*"Lost is cost!"*

*"Cost is Tost!"*

*"Tost is frost!"*

*"Frost is lost!"*

*"Yeaaaaaah!" they all squealed and giggled and spun around again.*

*"Can you help me?" the boy asked.*

*The four fairies stopped suddenly and flew back into a line.*

*"Help you? Help you what? Help you how? Help you why?"*

*More giggles.*

*"Could you help me find my way out of this place? So I can go home."*

*"Home?"*

*"Comb?"*

*"Dome?"*

*"Gnome?"*

*Giggles.*

*"Home," the boy said.*

*"You can't go home."*

*"Why not?"*

*"Because, silly! You are home!"*

*"You are comb!"*

*"You are dome!"*

*"You are gnome!"*

*"Yeaaaaaa!"*

*The boy stared up at the fairies, shook his head, and began to pull himself out of the pool."*

*"What are you doing?" asked Tibby, Libby, Vibby, and Gibby in unison.*

*"I'm leaving," he said as he pulled himself out of the pool and up onto the lip.*

*"No!"*

*"Bo!"*

*"So!"*

*"Wo!"*

*The boy rubbed his nose and ignored them. His clothes were soaked.*

*"You can't leave! You must stay!"*

*"Way!"*

*"Pray!"*

*"Gay!"*

*More giggles all around.*

*The boy stood and the fairies darted up and away. The boy looked around at the dense, dark trees.*

*"Can you at least tell me which way?" he said, now annoyed.*

*The fairies all looked at him and none said a word as though this might stop him.*

*"Fine," he said with a deep sigh. "I'll find my own way."*

*He scanned the trees that surrounded him for a few moments, then glanced back up at the fairies one last time. They had all disappeared again. He shrugged and shifted his gaze back to the forest.*

*The boy began to step down off the lip when suddenly, one of the fairies swooped down right before his eyes.*

*She batted her little eyes and tilted her head just so.*

*"Please don't go," she said in a soft, gentle, pleading voice. "We like you. We want you to stay."*

*She paused, fluttering her eyes and wings, and smiled sweetly.*

*"Please?"*

*The boy stared at her for a moment.*

*"I'm sorry," he said, "but I must leave."*

*The little fairy lowered her head and then shook it slowly.*

*"Tsk-tsk-tsk," she said. "You can't leave. And you won't. Because we will not let you."*

*With that, she looked up again. Her eyes had turned a reddish tint and her little smile had vanished. She looked up into the trees and nodded. Before the boy could even look, a vine noose quickly slipped around his neck and jerked him backward. He fell with a splash back into the pool and then, before he could push his way back to the surface, he felt the noose tightening around his neck once more, and he was pulled from the water.*

*He lifted up, slowly, his hands clutching the vine around this throat. He gasped and kicked his feet as they left the water below.*

*One of the fairies swooped before him and smiled.*

*"You can stay here forever and ever," she said. "And we'll play games and dance and sing and rhyme, too!"*

*"Moo!"*

*"Zoo!"*

*"Boo!"*

*Giggles.*

*"And when you're no fun anymore, we'll make a great wind chime out of your bones!"*

*"Stones!"*

*"Cones!"*

*"Moans!"*

*Giggles.*

*The boy's eyes had begun to bulge and he made raspy sounds from his throat.*

*"Bring him all the way up into the trees," one of the fairies said. "We can have fun with him there!"*

*The boy was lifted higher still, the trees above growing closer and closer, and the fairies giggling and giggling. He knew he had to act quickly, before he reached those trees. He reached down with one hand and felt the immediate searing of added pressure around his neck from the noose. But he didn't care—this was his only chance.*

*He reached for his katana and pulled it free, and with all his remaining strength swung it upwards, lashing out and hoping the blade would find its mark.*

*It did. The vine rope broke.*

*The boy fell back into the water with a mighty splash.*

# 46

They opened a door and walked down a long and narrow dark hall lit with low red lights, turned a corner, and slid aside a heavy dark curtain.

They were alone.

Clarence flashed a wide, almost mischievous, smile. His face and glasses tinted red in the glow of the bulbs as he unzipped his bag and pulled something out. He handed it to Jaden.

Jaden's eyes widened.

"This is—"

"*Spider-Man Reign*, issue number one," Clarence interrupted excitedly. "Black variant cover. One of the single rarest comics currently in existence. Yes, I know."

"Where'd you get this?" Jaden asked.

"A friend of a friend of a friend, who just happened to know someone who just happened to attend this year's San Diego Comic Con."

Jaden looked to Clarence then back at what he held.

"This is—"

"Awesome. Yes."

"How much did you pay for this?"

Clarence chuckled.

"That, you'll never know," he said. "Though let's just say my paper route just got a lot bigger."

"No, really, tell me."

Clarence paused, then leaned forward and whispered into his ear as though they were surrounded by others.

"You're crazy," Jaden said. "That's a lot of money."

"And you wouldn't have done the same?"

"That's beside the point," Jaden said, grinning.

"Exactly," Clarence said taking the comic back. "Exactly."

# 47

*... and sank down as though he were being sucked by a current. He was gripped with fear.*

*He fought and fought with all his might to push back toward the surface, kicking his legs and feet and thrusting up and out with his arms and hands. It was futile. He was sinking, down and down, into a dark, dark place. Once again, he thought it might be over, that he might sink into this darkness until he became just another part of it and nothing more. Air bubbles slipped from his nose and mouth.*

*And then, he was rising.*

*He kicked and swam with all his might, rising up and up, until he could see the faintest of light coming from the water above and he reached for this light as though it were life itself.*

*He broke the surface with a great gasp, and for a few long moments all he could do was breathe and breathe. When his lungs were again filled to capacity and the fear of what might have been subsided, he brushed his wet, blond hair from his eyes and blew the water from his nose.*

*He looked around. He was in a shaded place again. There were trees all around, as before, though not as many, and not as close. He again found himself in a clearing, but a smaller one—a manmade one. The light was that of predawn. There was a chilly breeze, and across the way he could see a small dirty yellow tent blowing with this breeze. But the boy's attention quickly fell to his immediate place within this clearing and for a moment he lost his will to breathe.*

*The boy was neck-deep in a body of water, in a large pot. Once the smells of the pot and what lay within the water came to him, he flinched and stood. He could see that the water in the pot was the color of blood, and was mixed with spices and other ingredients that floated to the surface: flesh, bone, and even hair, much of which stuck to his body like seaweed.*

*He jumped from the pot to the ground and looked back. The pot was only quarter his height. How he had stood in it was just another impossibility that had somehow happened. The pot sat on a smoldering fire of charred wood that was but embers. Had the fire been full on—had the stew been at a boil ...*

*For a moment, he just stood and breathed deeply, eyes closed, and tried not to think of what he had seen. For a moment, it seemed as though he might be able to put it out of his mind. But just then, he heard heavy footsteps nearby, coming fast. He didn't even have time to react before the meaty fist struck him hard in the face.*

*The boy sailed off his feet and landed on his back with a painful thud, knocking the air from his lungs. He opened his mouth and gasped, feeling the deep, searing pain in his chest. His eyes bulged as the figure that had just struck him stepped forward.*

*It was a big, burly man, tall with dark hair and a thick beard, who wore a checkered red and black shirt, big heavy boots, and dirty brown overalls. He eyed the boy intently, even angrily, and moved the large axe from his left shoulder to his right.*

*"Whadya doin' here?" he asked in a slow, simmering, drawl.*

*The boy could not answer. He was still gasping for air, and could do little more than stare.*

*"Huh? Ya gonna answer? Or I gonna hafta make ya?"*

*The man paused, eying the hilt of the katana that poked up over the boy's shoulder.*

*"Fine, don't speak," he said. "Don't matter none. We both know why ya here anyway, don't we? Yaa, another one spyin' on me, ain't ya? Ya spyin'!"*

*He nodded.*

*"Ohh, they send 'em young these days, don't they?" he continued. "Younger and younger. Think that makes a difference, they do. But it don't. No sir, no ma'am. It don't. Old, young, tall, small … it makes no difference. Ya spy on Big Red, ya end up big dead!"*

*The man chuckled at his own wit, but his grin quickly turned sour.*

*"Get up, spyin' boy. Ya and Big Red gonna dance."*

*When the boy made no move to stand, Big Red came forward and grabbed him by his hair and lifted him to his feet.*

*"Ya think ya all can outsmart me, eh?" he said. "Well, I'll show 'em and I'll show ya how smart Big Red can be."*

*Big Red turned and began to drag the boy across the opening, past the tent and passed the pot, and the boy grabbed at the man's thick, hairy forearms and kicked his feet, struggling to free himself from his grasp. But it made no difference.*

*"Here!" Big Red said, tossing the boy face-down on top of a tree stump and placing his heavy boot in the center of the boy's back.*

*The boy tried to squirm, but it was hopeless. Then he saw the blood-stained bucket just below his head, and instantly realized what was happening.*

*"Nooo!" he blurted as he saw the shadow of the axe rising high.*

*"What they gonna think when they see your spyin' little head starin' out at 'em from a sack?" Big Red said. "Huh? What they gonna say then?"*

*The axe rose to its peak.*

*"Wait!" the boy pleaded.*

*Big Red just sneered, as though the boy under foot was nothing more than a chicken. But then …*

*"What the hell that be? Huh?"*

*The boy stilled his squirm and felt Big Red's weight leaning forward over him.*

*"Huh? What that?" the behemoth repeated.*

*The boy noticed the small vial of green glowing liquid had fallen from his pocket during the struggle and lay on the ground a few feet away. It was glowing brightly.*

*"That yours? Huh?" Big Red asked, increasing his foot's pressure on the boy's back "Huh? Is it?"*

*"Yes," the boy near cried.*

*"What is it?"*

*No answer.*

*More pressure. "I said what is it?"*

*"… don't know … please …"*

*Big Red paused.*

*"Poison?" he asked. "That it? Poison?"*

*Still no answer.*

*"Ya tryin' to poison Big Red, that right?" Big Red said, increasing his pressure on the boy's back to an almost unbearable level. "That ya plan, is it? Is it?!"*

*But before the boy could answer, Big Red had reached down and snatched up the green glowing vial in his big, meaty hand. He stared at the vial for a moment.*

*"Poison," he concluded bitterly.*

*Big Red reached down and flipped the boy roughly to his back and pulled him into position on the stump, then sat atop the boy's chest, nearly crushing him. He grabbed the boy's hair and yanked his head up, staring down at him with hatred in his eyes.*

*"Ya spyin' devil," he said. "I'll teach ya good. Real good."*

*Big Red smashed the boy's head back to the trunk and began to unplug the top to the vial.*

*"Ya wanna poison Big Red? Well, Big Red wanna poison ya too."*

*He flipped the top off and tossed it aside. He clutched the boy's hair and held his head in place, and brought the vial down toward the boy's mouth.*

*"Open up, little spyin' boy. Open up real wide."*

*The boy clenched his mouth and kicked his legs and flailed his arms.*

*"Open!" Big Red shouted.*

*The boy clamped down his lips as though to eat them whole. Big Red let go of his hair, took him by the mouth, and squeezed hard, parting the boy's lips slightly.*

*Big Red poured the green liquid into the boy's mouth, then placed a vice-like hand over the boy's mouth and nose.*

*"Swallow!" he commanded.*

*The boy fought as long as he could, but his eyes began to bulge and he could no longer take it. He swallowed the liquid in one ugly gulp.*

*Big Red waited a few moments before he let go the boy and eased up off him. The boy clutched his throat, gagged, and rolled off the stump to the ground on his hands and knees, spitting and coughing.*

*"Don't like takin' ya own medicine, I see," Big Red sneered with delight. "Don't like it one little bit."*

*He waited.*

*"Do it hurt ya? Do ya insides feel like they bleedin' out? Do it make ya want to die? Huh? How's it makin' ya feel, spyin' boy?"*

*The boy had not moved since he hit the ground except for the slow rise and fall of his back.*

*Big Red stepped forward with his big axe.*

*"Ya dead yet?" he asked, nudging the boy with a heavy boot. "Huh?"*

*And it was then that the boy, this ronin boy, began to laugh, soft at first, then gradually louder, as though with revelation. The boy laughed and laughed.*

*"What's so funny?" Big Red asked.*

*And although there was anger in Big Red's voice, the boy could sense a hint of fear.*

*"Ya gone mad? That it?" Big Red asked as he gripped his axe. "Poison made ya mad as a loon?"*

*The boy's laugher was loud and hard.*

*Big Red's jaw clenched.*

*"Shut up!" he spat, and kicked the boy hard in the ribs.*

*The laughter did not stop, and so Big Red kicked the boy again, nearly lifting him clear off the ground. But still, the boy laughed on and on.*

*"I said shut up!" Big red shouted. "Ya hear shut up! Shut up or I'll take ya head I will! Take ya head!"*

*Big Red lifted his axe high.*

*"Shut up!"*

*The laughing stopped. The boy turned his head to face him. Big Red's axe was still perched at its peak, not moving.*

*Big Red stared into the face of the boy before him. The boy's face, neck, and eyes all seemed to be pulsing, throbbing veins.*

*The boy glared back through moppy, wet hair, his eyes near aflame with an inner-light. Then that same light flickered and the boy's eyes grew dark—very dark.*

*"Little demon!" Big Red yelled, and brought the axe down.*

*The boy rolled out of the way and sprung back up to his feet. He withdrew his katana and held it at the ready before him, and looked down upon his own throbbing, veiny hands. He squeezed the hilt in his hands and heard the wood moan with it.*

*Big Red was coming again, his axe arching for a strike. But the boy did not move from his position, waiting and watching as the axe arched higher still, and then came whizzing down.*

*The boy narrowed his eyes and cut out with his katana and met the axe. There was no parry. The axe splintered and shattered, and its steel head sliced the ground near the boy's feet as the katana's blade continued on through, tearing through fabric, then flesh, then blood, then bone, then fabric once more. The boy finished with a small twirl and brought his katana to his side, and stared at the man before him.*

*Big Red's arms fell to his sides. His mouth sagged open. His eyes were frozen in a moment of dumb and disbelief.*

*The top half of Big Red's body fell away from the bottom half and hit the ground with a bloody thud. His legs remained planted firmly on the ground.*

*The boy swallowed hard and took a deep breath. He stared at the standing legs before him before he felt something change and saw that the veins around his hands were shrinking back to normal. His heartbeat slowed and he felt as though a weight were being slowly put back upon him. Suddenly, he was exhausted. He looked around and saw Big Red's tent.*

*He forced himself forward and without thinking, and slowly began to make his way to it. He reached up, took hold of the zipper, and pulled it down.*

*Ziiiiiiiiiii—*

# 48

"So what's so cool about it?" Gloria asked. "It's just a comic."

"Just a comic?" Clarence said. "*Just a comic*? No. *Amazing Spider-Man* number 272 is just a comic. *Robin* number 41 is just a comic. But this—this is not just a comic, this is the holy grail!"

"I'm with Gloria on this one," Bill said taking a bite of his pepperoni pizza. "I may not know shit about comics or anything, but aren't, like, *Superman* number one or *Spider-Man* number one like the *real* holy grails of Dorkdom?"

"It's all relative," Clarence said. "Of course those comics are *the* comics, but they go for anywhere from a hundred thousand dollars and up. No one real can get their hands on those. You have to be a super-millionaire or something.

"But that," Clarence continued, pointing to the comic Jaden now held, "that is as good as it gets for the everyman."

"So in other words, it's junk," Gloria said, eliciting a whistle and a high-five from Bill.

"It's definitely not junk," Jaden said as he handed it back to Clarence. "*Definitely* not."

A few moments passed.

"Aren't you going to get something to eat?" Gloria asked Jaden.

"Nah, not hungry," he replied.

Gloria shrugged and took in a spoonful of yogurt.

"I believe," she said abruptly, "that there are only three kinds of people in the world."

"This should be interesting," Clarence said.

"And they all can be summed up by how they eat their yogurt," she added.

Bill laughed.

"Seriously," Gloria said. "I've given this a lot of thought."

"Clearly."

"Anyway, there are those who stir their yogurt, those who shake their yogurt, and those who dig. If you really think about it, it really says a lot about what kind of person you are. Like say, for example, I like to stir my yogurt. This means I'm careful, but not obsessive; fairly open-minded, but willing to try new things … branch out. See?"

"Yes," Bill said, shaking his head "no."

"And Clarence," Gloria continued, "I'll bet you like to dig your yogurt. Always one careful spoonful at a time, all the way to the bottom, am I right?"

"Actually," Clarence said, "that is how I eat yogurt."

"Of course it is," Gloria said "That's because you're a well-organized person who likes to fuss over details. And I'll bet anything that you're a shaker, Bill."

"And what would that say about me if I was?" Bill asked.

"It says that you're a person who knows what they want and isn't afraid to get messy or break a few rules along the way to get there," she replied. "Am I right, or am I right?"

Everyone looked at Bill.

"I do shake," he said with a shrug.

Everyone laughed.

"Okay, what about Jaden?" Bill asked "Which is he?"

Gloria looked across at Jaden, squinting.

"Honestly, I don't know," she said. "Jaden's always been kind of an enigma. A riddle. Aren't you Jaden?"

She smiled knowingly.

"Um, I guess," Jaden said.

"Well then, how *do* you eat your yogurt?" Clarence asked.

"I don't," Jaden replied. "I don't like yogurt."

# 49

*—iiiiiiiiiiiiip.*

*The sensation that followed was so overwhelmingly disorienting that the boy's mind could barely grasp it. For a moment, he was frozen in shock.*

*The boy blinked. He had been standing in an open clearing in the woods and had approached a tent, taken hold of its zipper, and pulled down, and had leaned forward to peek his head inside. And that is when things had changed again.*

*When he stuck his head inside the tent, he found himself facing a ceiling. When he tried to pull back out of the tent, he felt a wall behind him. He sat up.*

*Sat up? He had been standing not a second before, but now he was laying down, in a black bag with a long zipper that stretched down its center.*

*A shiver broke through him like a wave, followed by another and another. Suddenly, he felt sick. He pulled the zipper down farther and got out quick. He stood for a moment looking at the dark, ugly husk he had just exited. It lay on a steel table like a shed skin. He stood for a while just watching the body bag, half-expecting it to lunge for him, to take him back in.*

*A humming came to his ears. He was standing in a small place, a room no larger than a small bathroom. The walls were bare and steel, as was the floor and ceiling, and a single red light bulb hung high on the wall cast all in its bloody glow. Suddenly, it was very cold. The boy could see his breath.*

*He turned and saw a door and went to it. He took hold of the metallic lever and lifted, and the door cracked open. He pushed it with the edge of his katana and the door swung open into a small, dark room.*

*"Hello?" he said cautiously.*

*Silence.*

*He slid on his mask and at once could see clearly. The room was square with a metallic table in its center, and an empty stretcher beside it. The walls were lined with bottles of liquid and strange objects. He crossed the room to another door, on the other side of which was a long hallway, which stretched to another door at its far end. He walked down the hall, his katana drawn and ready, and opened the next door.*

*He was now standing in a wider hallway—a main hall—and he could see the many doors that branched off it. To the left, the hall stretched away to a distant set of double doors. To his right, just a few steps away, was a door with a sign above it that read "EXIT."*

*He stepped to the exit door, opened it, and found a stairwell crammed from floor to ceiling with chairs, tables, desks, cabinets, and stretchers. They were all piled with no order, as though they had been just thrown down from above as a sort of makeshift barricade.*

*It worked.*

*The boy shut the door and proceeded down the hall to the left.*

*He pushed through the double doors and found himself in a lobby. The floor was carpeted, and on the wall hung a painting of sheep grazing in a field. Beside the painting was a glass-encased bulletin board. One side of the bulletin was filled with the activities committee fieldtrips to ball games and plays, and related information. There was also a part for The Hundred Dollars Winner's Lottery. The other side of the bulletin board was dedicated to the employee of the month for June: a scrawny bald man named Jon Han, an environmental service worker. He was pictured cutting a cake in a group picture with, presumably, other environmental service workers. Jon Han had a big smile. On the glass before Jon Han's face was a hand print made of blood.*

*The lobby was very quiet. The boy swallowed and tightened his grip on the katana.*

*To his left was another set of double doors, and the sign above them read "Cafeteria."*

*He pushed open the doors and froze, and his hand quickly covered his nose.*

*It was indeed a cafeteria, but the tables and chairs were thrown around crazily, and often on-end. At the far end there was an overturned salad bar. A black mist of flies hovered near the ceiling like a storm cloud.*

*There was blood everywhere.*

*Suddenly, there came a rattling, clattering sound, like a metal cup or pan cover had hit the floor. The boy spun and looked in the direction of the sound: near an open doorway that he figured led to the kitchen.*

*"Hello?" he called out.*

*A head popped up from behind the salad bar. Then another, and another. And others, too.*

*Children.*

*The boy opened his mouth to say something, but before he could, the children began to growl and hiss. They were barely clothed. Their chests were exposed and discolored, brown and gray and bleeding. Even from such a distance, the boy could see the blood trickling from their open mouths. Their eyes were black. Suddenly, they sprang forward and raced toward him, wildly throwing chairs out of their path.*

*The boy turned and fled. He ran through the lobby until he reached another exit door and threw it open. The way was clear and he took the stairs up three at a time. He had barely reached the next landing when he heard the door burst open below and the growls and hisses of the mad children. He grabbed hold of the handle of the next door and pulled, but it was locked. The boy cursed and ran up the next flight to the next door and tried its handle.*

*Locked again.*

*He ran on, checking door after door. Every time, the doors were locked. He could hear the children a few flights below, still chasing him.*

*When he came to the last door, he paused, then took hold of the handle, pulled … it opened. He rushed inside and found himself in an open solarium. He could see outside through large glass windows. It was dark gray and raining. One of the windows had been broken and a rain-swept wind blew through the hole. The solarium floor was wet with rain and glass. It crunched beneath his feet and he almost slipped and fell. He looked around, still with the help of the illumination provided by his mask. He could see that the solarium was a dead end. One hall branching to his right was blocked with piled bed frames, and the way to his left stacked with old desks and medical equipment.*

*There was nowhere to go, and nowhere to hide.*

*That's when he saw the chute marked "Dirty Linen."*

*Without hesitation, he opened the chute and peered in. Inside was a dark hole, leading down.*

*Behind him, the first of the crazed children burst through the doorway.*

*Without looking back, the boy dove into the chute and fell downward, until his descent was stopped short by a blockage of linen. The linen was wet and smelly—the smell was horrendous. The chute was narrow, and he could barely move. He began to panic, thrashing and trying to push his way out. But he only slipped farther down into the chute. It was like quick sand, and he became entangled. He screamed.*

# 50

The library was very quiet.

Bill sat down at the table across from Jaden and began to rummage through his book bag.

"Been waiting all day for this," he said.

"Waiting for what?" Jaden asked, although he had an idea.

Bill pulled the porno magazine from his bag. He eyed Jaden and raised his eyebrows, then ripped open the protective plastic and flipped the magazine open to its approximate middle.

"Whoa!" he said and whistled.

Then, remembering where he was, he whistled again, this time much softer.

"Check those out!" he said in a hushed whisper, and turned the magazine so that Jaden could see.

Jaden stared at the naked women before him impassively.

"She's got big boobs." Jaden stated.

"Uh, yeah!" Bill said turning the page. "Oh man! Jeez, look at those! What I wouldn't give ..."

He shook his head and began flipping pages at random.

"Psst!" Jaden said, nodding toward the librarian, who was making her way across the library toward them.

Bill quickly hid the magazine beneath the table around his lap.

"Boys," the librarian said in a way that spoke for her ability to spot and squash potential mischief-makers. Then she passed their table and was gone down an aisle of books.

The magazine was back in front of Bill almost as soon as she passed.

"You act like you've never seen a girl before," Jaden said.

"Not like this—well, at least for a while."

He turned a page and a satisfied smile crept to his lips.

"Mom caught me on the computer the other day," he said. "She cut off my Internet privileges for a month."

"You were watching porn on the Internet?"

"Yeah, what else is there?"

Jaden watched him for a moment. Then his eyes shifted to a group of girls entering the library.

"You know what you might find better than girls in a magazine?" Jaden asked.

"What?" Bill replied, only slightly paying attention.

"The real thing."

Bill looked up and Jaden nodded toward the library's entrance.

"Sara Pacouchy," Bill said aloud.

"Yup."

Jaden reached across the table and slid over the magazine and began leafing through it.

"Oh man … she's so hot," Bill said.

"And she's coming right for us …" Jaden said in a whispered and conspiratorial tone as the group of girls drew close.

Jaden covered the magazine with his book bag as the girls drew even with the table.

Sara Pacouchy sneezed.

"Envy," Bill said.

When the girls all turned to him with peculiar expressions on their faces he flushed and said, "Ah, I mean bless you."

The girls looked at each other and laughed, and moved on.

"That was smooth," Jaden said, stifling a laugh.

Bill shook his head and muttered something to himself.

"It's not that bad," Jaden said leafing through the magazine. "You should talk to her. Ask her out."

Bill sighed.

"Yeah right," he said. "Like she'd ever wanna talk to someone like me."

"Maybe she would. How do you know?"

"Until *that* moment, she hasn't made eye contact with me since like the eighth grade."

"Probably because she likes you. Probably shy or something."

"She ain't shy, trust me."

"What's that supposed to mean?" Jaden asked as he reached the centerfold and turned the magazine sideways to take it all in.

"It means she's a slu—" Bill caught himself.

"She's a what?" Jaden asked with a touch of amusement in his voice.

When Bill didn't answer, Jaden looked up and saw Bill biting his lower lip, his eyes open wide. Jaden turned in his seat to see Mrs. Covey, the school librarian, standing directly behind him.

# 51

*For a moment the cow simply grazed in the grass. Then it lifted its head and mooed.*

*The tip of the katana poked through the soft flesh of the cow's underbelly, and then began to slide and cut. Finally, the boy fell from the cow's stomach as though born of it, and hit the ground in a stew of blood and innards. The cow toppled sideways and didn't move again.*

*The boy stood, his body covered in a sick wetness. He bent over and vomited.*

*Finally, he straightened up and wiped his mouth, then he tried to clear some of the muck from his face and hair.*

*It was hopeless.*

*He stood there for a moment looking at the vast graveyard around him. Then his legs buckled and he collapsed to the ground in a seated heap, his legs folded beneath him. And for a long-long time he just sat there. Soon, flies began to circle and settle on him. It began to rain.*

# 52

"A week's detention!" Clarence said as he undressed. "Your parents are gonna flip!"

Jaden shrugged.

"So what happened to the magazine?" Clarence asked.

"She ripped it in half," Jaden replied. "Made it real dramatic-like. Said, 'Trash belongs in the trash!' Then she threw it away."

"Bet she taped it back together when you left. Reading through it right now!"

"Let's go, ladies!" Coach Pikes said as he strode through the locker room. "I want everyone poolside in two minutes."

Jaden pulled up his shorts and tightened the drawstring. Coach Pikes stopped in front of him.

"Quitting are you?" Coach Pikes asked.

"Huh?"

"The team. You've quit?"

Jaden looked across the locker room and made eye contact with Joshua, who was eyeing him intently.

"I was told you cut me," Jaden replied.

"How can I cut you if you never show up for practice?" the coach asked. "So? Are you in or out?"

"I really don't think I'm big enough, or—"

"Big-smig, you're fast. Only lugheads need be big. You've got speed, you don't get hit, and if you don't get hit, then you don't need to be big, see?"

"I guess."

"Look Jaden," Coach Pikes said in a more serious tone, "You have got natural talent on that field. This I know. What I *don't* know, and what *you* don't know, and what *nobody* may ever know, is just how talented you can be. No practice, no play. So what do you say? Do I get to see you in pads today?"

"Today?"

"Next practice. Four o'clock sharp."

Jaden paused, then smiled.

"I'll think about it."

Coach Pikes smiled.

"Good. I'll be looking forward to seeing you," Coach Pikes said as though that settled everything.

Then he turned to leave and pointed at another student.

"Hey, Burner, wash that grease out of your hair," he said. "I don't want you dirtying up my pool again."

Everyone in the locker room laughed.

# 53

*When he finally stood, the rain had washed away most all the cow innards that had covered him.*

*He looked around.*

*It was growing dark, and the graveyard he was in was on a sloping hillside. Already, small muddy rivers of water were cascading down around him.*

*He began to make his way down the slope, slowly and cautiously, and had gone a fair distance when the thunder erupted in the sky so loud that the boy had to cover his ears. Suddenly, lightning struck the headstone before him and shattered it in an explosion of debris. He dove and began to slide down the hill.*

*The ground was too muddy to stop. He was trying hard to stabilize himself when he slid headlong into an open grave.*

# 54

They stood poolside in shorts and bathing suits as Coach Pikes recorded attendance on an old clipboard. When he got to Jaden, he winked.

On one side of Jaden was Clarence, on the other was Gloria. She wore a bathing suit and her face was washed clean of makeup. Her hair hung straight down around her shoulders.

"I think I'm going to be sick," she said.

"Why, what's wrong?" Jaden asked.

She stuck out her tongue.

"You took it out?"

Gloria nodded.

"When?"

"Just now. In the locker room. But ever since, I can taste something funny in my mouth, like bile."

"Now ladies and germs," Coach Pikes said lowering his clipboard, "today we work the board."

A murmur of excitement passed among the students.

"Okay, calm down, calm down. Let's not drown ourselves in tears of joy. There'll be plenty of time for that later," he said, gesturing toward the pool and drawing a few chuckles.

"We'll do this in alphabetical order," he added, looking down at his clipboard. "Mr. Alsup. Would you?"

"For two-hundred million dollars," Clarence whispered as he eyed the water, "would you jump into a pool full of razors?"

"Probably not," Jaden replied.

"Gloria?"

"I'd rather not think about it, actually," she whispered.

"How long do I have to stay in?" Jaden asked.

"You don't," Clarence said. "You can get out as fast as you can. *If* you can."

"Exactly," Jaden said. "Hmmm … probably loose a lot of blood …"

Jaden eyed the pool, deep in thought.

"… or sink to the bottom," Clarence added.

"If I couldn't get out, could I then forfeit the money and have someone help me to get out?"

"No," Clarence replied. "It's all or nothing."

"No way, then."

They all watched as the brown-haired boy jumped off the board and into the pool with a small splash.

"How about if there was just one poisonous snake and all you have to do is swim from one side to the other?" Clarence asked.

"Where's the snake?"

"That's the thing, you don't know where. It could be anywhere. All the way at the bottom, on the far side … you could swim the whole way ten times over and never come into contact with it."

"So you're saying it doesn't necessarily want to bite you?" Jaden asked.

"That's right."

"But obviously, if provoked, it will."

"That's right."

Jaden and Gloria looked at each other.

"I'd do it," Jaden said.

"Never," Gloria said.

"Oh, what would you be thinking" Clarence said, "the moment you jumped in when that snake's right on top of you?"

"I'd kick it," Jaden said.

Clarence laughed.

"You can't kick a snake. I'd bite you so quick!"

They watched as another boy jumped.

"All right, what if there was an alligator?"

# 55

*The boy couldn't breathe.*

*The wind had been knocked out of him, and for a moment, he could not move, either. He lay face-down atop a wooden casket. All around him, he could hear the sounds of pooling water falling into the grave. And there was another sound, too.*

*He finally sat up. The casket he was straddling had cracked in the middle, but had not caved in. He looked up. The grave seemed deep and the walls were wet with mud and other living things. As he tried to gather himself, two worms fell from the sides of the grave and landed with sickly, slimy thuds on the casket not an arm's reach away.*

*He shivered.*

*The rushing water continued to pool over the edge of the grave like a miniature stream emptying into a deep, black canyon. Water was already rising around the sides of the casket and would undoubtedly soon swallow it up. The boy balanced himself and stood up slowly. Even standing he was still about two head-lengths below ground. He had lost a sandal in the fall and it was nowhere to be seen. He kicked off the remaining sandal and as he did, he realized that he no longer was in possession of his katana. He must have lost it when he fell. He looked down, searching, peering into the murky-black water that was rising around the casket sides like the ocean around a capsized ship.*

*The boy frowned and crouched back down to the casket. Another worm fell just short of his toes.*

*He didn't bother to roll up his sleeve as he reached into the pooling water; it was already too wet for that. He groped around for a while, but found nothing. He tried the other side—still no luck.*

*He stood up again. By now, the water had begun to rise over the sides of the casket, closing in around it. The boy's feet were now immersed in water. He looked up to the ground's edge for a moment, as rain pelted his face, and then after another moment, he took two running steps and lunged for an edge. He met it halfway up his chest and clung there, half in, half out of the grave, like a man perched on the edge of a cliff.*

*Then he saw his katana. It was resting a few feet away in the sagging grass. The boy tried to pull himself up with his hands and arms, digging his toes and feet into the earth walls of the grave. His fingers meet grass and pulled, but the soil came loose in two clumps, and he began to slide back down again. He dug his feet for a hold, but the walls of the grave were too muddy and loose—worse, even than the ground above.*

*He slipped back down into the grave and landed on his knees with a loud crack and splash. He cried out in pain even as he steadied himself atop the casket. He looked down and saw that he had smashed in a small portion of the casket's top. Water was beginning to swirl into the fist-sized hole he had made. The boy stood and kicked the mud from his feet, then noticed with a chill that part of what he kicked away was moving on its own.*

*It was a rat. Then more rats came, scurrying out of the hole in the casket.*

*Water continued to cascade in from above.*

*The boy lunged against the side of the grave again, this time reaching a little farther out than before. Most of his lower body still hung below the ground, but his arms had reached out farther this time. He grasped for grass and mud—and for his katana—and clawed his feet into the muddy grave wall, and hung there for a moment. But then the grass in his fists began to uproot, and his feet again sank into the mud walls as though he was being devoured. He tried mightily to regain his hold, but that only quickened his fall as two mucky clumps of earth came loose and he lost his hold. He slid back into the grave like a giant's tongue back into its upturned mouth. His face and chest rubbed into the wall and this time when he landed, his feet were completely immersed. The water in the grave was now ankle-deep.*

*The boy looked down. The casket had disappeared from sight under the water. All he could see were the rats swimming maddeningly. Something latched onto the boy's leg. Startled, he jumped, then reached down and gripped the rat between his fingers, pulled it from him, and then threw it hard against the grave's far wall. It hit with a little smack and fell to the water, where it immediately began to swim frantically back toward him.*

*Instantly, a second rat was at his arm. He ripped it away and lunged for the edge of the hole, but as he did, his pants ripped and pulled at him. He looked back and saw that a part of his pants was now caught in the casket. He jerked his pants free, tearing them more, then again lunged for a corner of the grave. He perched there and frantically began to reach and claw and climb out of the pit.*

*He grasped and clawed and dug his feet over and over as water rushed into his face. Some of it flooded into his gasping mouth and he gagged and sputtered as he reached and dug some more. Below him, he could hear the terrified squeaks of the rats. It sounded like more than a few now.*

*The grass at his fingers kept ripping away, sending clumps of mud flying about. But the boy kept grasping, unwilling to relinquish his precarious hold. Already his feet had dug a large pock in the wall of the grave, but he could still not gain enough traction or leverage to climb out.*

*Thunder shook the earth with ear-splitting fury and the boy again lost his hold and slid back down. He landed so hard this time that he felt the casket give way beneath him with a sickening crack. His feet broke through and in he went. The boy was now up to his waist in water, and he could feel unseen rats scurrying around and into him. He felt something hard and scaly at his bare feet. He tried to step up out of the casket, but his leg was lodged between something. He pulled and flailed, slightly losing his balance. He felt two rats grab hold of his sleeve, and something was now crawling into his hair.*

*He waved his arms crazily and began to scream as a flash of lightning lit up the night sky and the grave like a nightmare.*

*Rats were everywhere.*

*The water kept rushing in. He pulled his foot, and pulled and pulled. He could feel his skin tearing as he screamed and fell back into the water, where he was now completely submerged.*

# 56

Almost half the students had made their jumps by the time Jaden stepped up onto the diving board. He walked out to its edge and stood there for a moment looking down at the clear water below.

"Anytime you're ready," Coach Pikes said.

Jaden bounced once, twice, then leapt out into the air. He extended his body full and long and dove down into the water. He sunk down, then spun and made his way back up to the surface. When he surfaced, everyone was clapping and cheering.

"Good job, Jaden! Good job! Hell of a dive!" Coach Pikes said as he turned to the others. "I told you he was a natural athlete!"

A few girls whistled and giggled. Jaden blushed and climbed out of the pool.

"Mrs. Lovely," Coach Pikes said, motioning for Gloria to go next.

Gloria hesitated, then walked to the short ladder. She climbed up, and slowly and cautiously walked to the edge of the board.

"Get ready for a tidal wave," Joshua said, followed by a smattering of laughter.

"Grow up, Mr. Burner." Coach Pikes said, although his tone suggested that he, too, was a little amused.

Gloria stood on the edge the board staring down. Her face seemed to have slackened, and she looked paler than usual.

"Anytime, Mrs.—"

Gloria threw up.

Coach Pikes helped her down off the board and back to the bleachers, where he knelt down and talked to her quietly for a few moments. Then he stood and addressed the class.

"I'll be taking Gloria to the nurse's office," he said. "There'll be no more dives today."

There were a few groans of protest.

"Class is close to done anyway. Everyone hit the showers and wait outside in the lobby until the bell. Okay?"

The students nodded.

Coach Pikes helped Gloria to her feet and slowly led her out of the pool area.

# 57

*Now there was complete darkness. Gone was the wetness. Gone was the rain.*

*Gone was the grave.*

*For a long time the boy sat in this darkness, silent and unmoving. Then a light came on high in the ceiling—a very bright light—and the boy was blinded by it. He shut his eyes and turned his head away. Eventually, he began to flutter his eyes open and managed to squint at his surroundings. He was in a small square room. The walls, floor, ceiling, even the door, were white and padded. He was held in a white jacket, his hands crisscrossed and bound to him.*

*He no longer had his katana, nor his mask. The only other thing in the room with him was a little black box on the other side.*

*He stared at this box for a long moment. He moved, pushing his legs, managing after an awkward moment or two to slide up the padded wall into a standing position.*

*He stood there for a few moments, eyeing the box, then slowly stepped forward until he was standing before the door and the black box.*

*The boy nudged the box with his foot and there was a sound from within it as though something had moved. He nudged it again, this time harder, and something inside the box slid from one side to the other. The boy hesitated for a long moment, then kicked the box over. It had no bottom and easily bounced away.*

*He stared down at what was left behind.*

*It was a small seashell, no larger than his fist.*

*The boy's eyes narrowed as he bent and crouched.*

*"What?" he breathed near inaudibly.*

*The shell twitched. Startled by this, the boy fell backward to his backside and quickly rolled to his side and looked at the shell.*

*It sat motionless for a moment, before something fell from the seashell's opening and landed on the white padded floor with a tiny tap.*

*It was a little black spider, no larger than a fingernail.*

*The boy gasped.*

*Another spider fell from the shell. Then another, and another.*

*The boy's eyes widened and he began to slide away until he reached the far wall, the corner.*

*Two more spiders fell from the shell to join the others, which were slowly making their way across the padded floor toward him.*

*Tap-tap-tap-tap. He could actually hear their tiny legs pattering across the padded floor.*

*More spiders fell. Three at a time. Then four more.*

*They fell and scurried over one another, and then came his way along with the rest.*

*Tap-tap-tap-tap-tap-tap-tap-tap.*

*A choked sound of horror escaped the boy's throat. He pushed deep into the corner as far as he could go.*

*Tap-tap-tap-tap-tap-tap-tap-tap.*

*"No!" the boy heard himself blurt.*

*Tap-tap-tap-tap-tap-tap-tap-tap.*

*The spiders were pouring out from the shell now like water from a faucet.*

*"Please ..."*

*The first of the spiders had reached him, and he managed to kick out at it and squirm away from it at the same time.*

*The seashell began to rock and bounce, and suddenly, a far larger spider popped out of its hole and landed upside down on the padding with a little thud. It quickly righted itself and scurried forward, toward him.*

*Pop-pop-pop-pop.*

*Spiders kept spilling out, big and small. Some flew out from the shell, like popcorn, and hit the far wall and were instantly up again, crawling.*

*Suddenly, the shell became still. A few seconds passed.*

*Without warning, a long, hairy spider leg slowly poked from the opening. It stretched and stretched—the length of an arm—then touched the floor. Another leg followed, and another, and after four enormous legs had emerged, the body of the spider began to wriggle through. It was large and hairy, its many eyes as big and black as marbles. It stared at the boy as it pulled its remaining four legs free of the shell.*

*It darted for the boy wildly.*

*The boy screamed.*

*The shell continued to pop and tap.*

*And then, everything went dark again ...*

# 58

Jaden stood beneath the water flow of the shower washing the chlorine from his hair and body. The water was hot, and steam clouds wafted about in curling waves.

Suddenly, Jaden heard laughter. He turned and saw Joshua and a few other football players entering the shower area.

"Why does he always shower in his shorts?" someone said mockingly, eyeing Clarence.

"Because he has no dick."

"He's just a fag."

"Hiding a boner."

"Leave him alone," Jaden said.

"Why, you in love?"

"Shut up."

"Think you touched a nerve."

"Maybe we should leave 'em alone so they can get busy."

"Just shut up."

"Awwwwwwww."

"Clarence and Jaden sitting in a tree. K-I-S-S-I-N-G!"

"Shut up."

"Make me."

"Blow me."

"Bet you'd like that."

More laughter.

"Where you going?" Joshua said, holding out his arm to stop Clarence from leaving.

Clarence looked at the shower floor.

"I said leave him alone, Josh."

"Leave the little *faggot* alone? Why? If I don't, he'll call Spider-Man to stop me?" Joshua said as he flashed a comic book he was hiding behind his back.

"Hey!" Clarence yelled. "That's mine!"

"Oh, is it? It was just lying on the floor, and I don't see your name on it anywhere."

"It's mine! You stole it out of my bag! Give it back!"

Clarence grabbed for it, but Joshua held it high out of his reach.

"Give it back," Jaden said.

"I don't know," Joshua said. "I was thinking about taking it out of its protective covering and just reading it here in the shower."

He started to open the plastic bag containing the book.

"Don't!" Clarence screamed. "Please, don't! *Don't*!"

"Joshua, give it back to him," Jaden said.

He started to step forward, but the other boys stood between him and Joshua.

"I'll tell you what," Joshua said to Clarence. "I'll give it back if you say you're a homo."

"Joshua!" Jaden said. "Stop!"

"Shut up, this doesn't concern you," Joshua said, then turned to Clarence. "Just say it and it's yours."

Clarence's face flushed, and his eyes began welling up with tears.

"I'm a homo," he whispered.

"What? I didn't catch that."

"I'm a homo."

"What?"

"I'm a homo," Clarence said again, and began to cry. "Now give it back."

"Hmmm, I bet if you're a homo," Joshua said. "That must mean you like to suck big cocks, don't you?"

Clarence nodded, head bowed.

"Say it."

"I like to suck cocks," Clarence said dejectedly.

"Big cocks."

"Big cocks," Clarence added.

More laughter.

Jaden muttered something and all heads turned toward him. The only sound was that of the falling water.

"What'd you just say?" Joshua asked, leaning in.

"I said, *you're* the fag," Jaden said defiantly.

The showers exploded with laughter and catcalls.

Joshua turned red in the face. He pushed Jaden hard.

Just then, the fire alarm sounded. There was a slight hesitation, and then Joshua quickly slipped the comic from its plastic and threw it hard into the showers, where it landed in a jet of wet. Then everyone returned to the lockers and hurried to get dressed.

Clarence gathered up his wet comic and ran back to his locker and stuffed it back in his bag. He got dressed quickly and quietly, without even bothering to towel off. Moments later, he was gone, before Jaden even had his pants on.

Jaden tightened his drawstring and slipped his tee shirt on. He stepped into his sneakers and tied them quickly. He could hear the other students already leaving the locker room. He slung his backpack over his shoulder and began to make his way to the exit.

A football player, wearing a jersey with the number 56, stepped in front of the door and blocked his path.

"Where you off to, pretty boy?" he said.

Jaden turned. Joshua and two other boys—numbers 8 and 44—stepped out into sight. Jaden looked around, and Joshua flashed a shark-like grin.

"It's just us," Joshua said.

Jaden tried to make a run for it. He darted back the way he had come, but was soon cut off. The other boy, number 56, stepped in behind him.

"You're not going anywhere," Joshua said, earning agreeing nods from the others.

"The fire alarm—" Jaden said. It was still ringing.

"What, you afraid of a little alarm? Is that it?"

The other boys laughed.

"Afraid you gonna catch fire and burn up? That what the little faggot thinks?"

Joshua glared at Jaden, almost daring him to do something.

"What puts out a fire?" Joshua asked aloud. "Water. Grab him!"

Jaden tried to push past number 56, but the boy was far bigger than he was, and held him up just long enough for the others to reach him.

"Leave me alone!" Jaden yelled. "I didn't do anything to you! I didn't do anything!"

Jaden thrashed and pushed and struggled as the others converged on him.

"Help!" Jaden yelled and then even louder. *"Help!"*

But the alarm drowned out his pleas.

Joshua punched him hard in the stomach. Jaden doubled over.

"Grab him, and bring him out back!" Joshua said.

"Yeah bring the faggot out back!" others agreed. "Yeah!"

They grabbed Jaden by his legs and arms and began to carry him away. He started crying, and was dumped by the toilet stalls. He hit the floor like a sack, and someone kicked him.

Jaden curled into a ball.

"Hold him there!" Joshua said. "Watch this!"

Joshua kicked open the stall door and lifted up the toilet seat with his foot. He unzipped his pants and peed into the toilet, and started laughing. His fellow football players laughed, too. Once he finished, Joshua zipped up and turned back to Jaden.

"Get him up! Bring him in here!" he commanded.

The others reached down and pulled Jaden up. Jaden tried to fight, kicking and screaming, but someone grabbed him by the hair and pulled hard. He cried out in pain, and before he could do anything to free himself, he was inside the stall.

Joshua straddled the toilet itself and took hold of Jaden's hair. He pulled him the last bit forward.

"There's a fire! There's a fire!" Joshua shouted mockingly. "Oh my god, the little faggot's on fire! Put him out! Put him out!"

Jaden screamed for help—a desperate, throat-scarring scream.

Joshua grabbed two fistfuls of hair and forced Jaden's head down into the toilet, silencing him.

The football players laughed and laughed.

# 59

*. . . and suddenly the room was filled with water. The boy's head dipped below the surface mid-scream, swallowing some. He coughed and sputtered, and kicked wildly to propel himself to the surface. He gagged and spat and coughed, and continued to kick his feet to stay afloat. All around him, he could feel the spiders. They were in his hair and on the back of his neck. A big one he smacked from his face and he began to scream again.*

*After a few moments, he realized he was back in the well where this nightmare had begun, the walls slippery and close around him.*

*A light appeared above, followed by the silhouette of a person peering down at him.*

*The boy screamed up at the figure, begging and pleading. But the figure disappeared from view, and the boy let loose his most throat-searing scream of all. It echoed up the well and rained back down on him. He began to claw at the walls, trying desperately to climb out. But his hands could find nothing to grip, and he only slipped and slipped. Still, he scratched and clawed frantically, and a few of his finger nails broke away. But he did not stop. He clawed and clawed, and wailed in anguish and torment.*

*Finally, a rope tumbled down into the well and hit him in his upturned face. He grabbed it and clung to it for dear life, and he began to climb. As he climbed, a peculiar laughter joined his sobs as he did. The spiders still clung to him by the dozens, and now that his hands were no longer free to brush them from his face, they crawled there eagerly.*

*Up he went, eyeing the light above, one grasping, clenched fist after another. As soon as he reached the top, he pulled himself out and over the edge. He hit the floor in a wet, hairy heap, and started to roll around, smacking wildly at the spiders that still clung to him. His smacks were hard and he clawed at his skin to strip the spiders from his body. He stomped them and clawed his skin some more, and ripped them from his head, even pulling clumps of his own hair by the fistful. He screamed and screamed, and smacked and clawed and ripped, as his skin and face grew dark with flowing blood. But he would not stop.*

*Finally, he fell to his knees, exhausted, and began to hug himself, weeping and shaking, his eyes darting this way and that. He even laughed a little, relieved that he was still alive and finally free of spiders. His teeth chattered and he bit his tongue. Blood flowed from his mouth.*

*From the shadows stepped a tall figure, who came forward and stood before the boy at his feet.*

*"What is your name child?" the figure asked in a soft voice.*

*The boy shook and wept and laughed, and did not even look up.*

*"I ask again, what is your name?"*

*Again, no response.*

*The man knelt and took the boy's chin in his hand and turned his head to face him. The boy's eyes were wild, frantic.*

*"What is your name?"*

*No answer.*

*The man reached into his robes and withdrew a glowing orb. He held it in front of the boy.*

*The boy stared into the orb, his eyes wide, transfixed. A long moment passed.*

*"What is your name?" the man asked once more.*

*"J-Ja-Jaden."*

*The boy still trembled and sobbed, but his laughter had ceased.*

*"Say it again," the man said in a compassionate tone.*

*"J-Jaden."*

*The man smiled and stood. He went to the door and opened it.*

*"Do what you must," the man said softly, and left the room, shutting the door behind him.*

*For a long time, the boy sat motionless and alone. Then he rose to his feet, went to the entrance, and hesitantly opened the door.*

# 60

"Settle down," Mrs. McDonald said as everyone walked into the classroom, still laughing. "We've already lost most of the class time due to the drill."

She had just began to take a visual attendance when she saw Jaden carrying his guitar case and making his way to his desk, without a word or eye contact with anyone.

Mrs. McDonald watched him curiously for a moment, then stepped in front of her desk.

"We probably have time for one, maybe two, speeches," she said, leaning back against her desk. "Any brave volunteers? Or is it alphabetical process of elimination as usual?"

Silence.

"As expected—"

Jaden raised his hand.

"Jaden? You're volunteering?"

He nodded.

In the back of the class, Joshua muttered something and those around him snickered.

"Well, this is a first," Mrs. McDonald said, stepping aside and motioning to the front of the class.

"The floor is all yours, Jaden."

Jaden stood and walked to the front of the room. Mrs. McDonald took a seat a few rows back and opened a notebook. She scribbled something, then folded her hands before her—the pen between them—and nodded for Jaden to began.

Jaden leaned his case against the blackboard, picked up a piece of chalk, and began to write on the board.

He wrote "Samurai," then placed the piece of chalk back and turned to the class.

"Does anyone know what a Samurai is?" he asked in a calm, soft voice.

A few hands went up. Jaden pointed to a girl in the front.

"Aren't they, like, oriental fighters or something?" she said.

"They're the ones that fight the ninjas on Saturday morning cartoons, right?" Joshua blurted, drawing laughter from about half the class.

Mrs. McDonald turned in her seat and glared at Joshua.

"Raise your hand," she said, clearly annoyed. "Please continue, Jaden."

"Yes," Jaden continued, "they were fighters. Warriors, really. And they were oriental—Japanese, actually. They were very prominent in the seventeen and eighteen hundreds. They were the defenders of their land. Their people. Their beliefs. Their honor. And they fought in fierce battles over said land and said people and said beliefs. And most importantly, over their honor."

"Wasn't a lot of them gay, too?" Joshua said, earning more laughter.

"After class," Mrs. McDonald said, pointing angrily at Joshua. "And one more remark, and you'll be spending the rest of this period in Mr. White's office. Understand?"

Joshua turned red and slouched down in his seat. His eyes narrowed to slits.

"No, it's okay," Jaden said. "Actually, there were quite a few queer Samurais in their time. It was a far different culture then and certain things were more widely accepted at the time. They also wore these loose-fitting pants called 'hakimas.' They were fairly baggy, sort of like the pants I'm wearing now. You might even say Samurais were like trendsetters or something. Like the first ravers."

Jaden did a little jig and began to hop.

The class chuckled. Mrs. McDonald, too. She nodded thoughtfully and began to write on her paper. She looked up at Jaden and smiled encouragingly.

"But more seriously," Jaden said, walking back to the blackboard, "the Samurai were great warriors. They fought in a time before guns or any of the modern technology we have today. They fought with …"

Jaden wrote "Katana" on the blackboard, then again faced the class.

"Does anyone know what a katana is?" he asked.

Hands shot up, many more than before. Jaden pointed to a boy in the back.

"It's a sword," the boy said.

Jaden nodded. "Yes. A katana is a sword."

He walked to his guitar case and knelt down before it. He unlatched it and opened it. And when he stood up again, an interested murmur rippled throughout the classroom.

"This is a katana," Jaden said, holding the sword out before him, twisting it around for the class to see. "It's held in a protective casing known as a scabbard or sheath. This end here is where it's gripped. It's known as the hilt."

He pulled on the hilt and withdrew the blade from its scabbard with a metallic *shhhhink*.

The class murmured its approval.

Mrs. McDonald nodded and wrote some more. Then she shut the notebook and placed her pen down and folded her hands before her. She smiled, clearly eager for more information.

"Is that real?" asked a girl up front.

"It is real and very sharp. And very, very old, actually."

Mrs. McDonald raised her hand.

"Yes?"

"Where did you get it?"

"It belonged to my grandfather," Jaden said. "He used to travel a lot, before his stroke I mean, and he bought this on one of his trips to Japan."

"When was this?"

"He wasn't even married then, so I'd say like sixty years ago at least."

"So this katana you hold is at least sixty years old?"

Jaden nodded.

"Yeah," he said. "Though it's probably much older because of some markings it's got on the hilt. My grandfather tried to explain that once, but I wasn't really interested at the time."

"But you are now."

Jaden grinned. "Yeah, I definitely am now."

"Very interesting, Jaden." Mrs. McDonald said. "Continue."

Jaden licked his lips.

"Right … well, like I said, it's pretty sharp and all, but if anyone wants to come up and hold it, they can."

Nearly every hand went up.

"Only a few," Mrs. McDonald said.

Jaden pointed to three students and they came to the front. In turn, they each took hold of the katana and cut through the air with it.

"Careful," Mrs. McDonald said more than once.

When they were finished, the last student handed it back to Jaden and returned to his seat.

Mrs. McDonald suddenly sprung from her seat.

"What the heck," she said. "Let me try."

And Jaden handed it to her.

"Wow," she said, moving it around. "It's far lighter than I thought it would be."

"Again that's probably because it's so old. It's authentic. Anything you might buy now—new—would be a lot heavier."

"And why is that?"

"Craftsmanship, I guess," he replied. "Anything made today is more often than not just for show and not made for actual battle. No thought goes into the weight of it, or the lack thereof, because it's an unnecessary detail."

Mrs. McDonald stabbed the air with a dramatic little flourish and the class laughed.

"Well," she said self-mockingly, "maybe in another lifetime."

She handed the katana back to Jaden and returned to her seat.

Jaden returned to the blackboard and wrote "Ronin."

"Does anyone know what a ronin is?"

No hands went up.

"A ronin is a Samurai without master," he said. "Dishonored. Shamed. An outcast. Any mark against one's honor could make one ronin. To become ronin was widely considered the lowest a Samurai could become. To become ronin was often a death sentence."

"How so?" Mrs. McDonald asked.

"Well, honor was such an important thing to the Samurai," Jaden replied. "Perhaps *the* most important thing. Like I said, battles—whole wars—were started over it. And so if someone's honor was tainted so much that they were considered ronin, well, they were often killed or …"

Jaden walked back to the board and wrote "Seppuku."

"Any idea what seppuku is?" he asked.

A few students raised their hands along with Mrs. McDonald.

Jaden pointed to a boy up front.

"It's when they kill themselves right?" the boy said.

"Right," Jaden said. "That's exactly it. Seppuku is the Samurai's traditional act of suicide. Samurais believed so highly in the honor of oneself that they often believed the only way for a ronin to regain his lost honor was in the act of suicide. It was the ultimate display of remorse, repentance, and dedication. They would stab themselves with their own katanas—stick their very blades into their own flesh—and end their own lives. They believed honor lost in life could be restored in death."

Jaden paused and looked out the side window, the katana at his side. It was snowing steady now.

"Ronin would often sneak onto the battlefield just for a chance to die a more honorable death," he continued. "And it was said that ronin were some of the fiercest warriors the world has ever known."

He turned back to the class but his gaze was on the floor, at his feet.

"Do you know why?" he asked, then paused. "Because a person who has nothing more to lose can fight freely. Calmly. Without hesitation or doubt. A person who's staring death in the face, regardless of the outcome, is a person without restraint. Without fear."

Jaden again knelt down to his guitar case and took something from it, then stood.

"And this is a mask," he said holding the mask up for all to see. "Samurai wore thick armor, and masks were a part of their defense. But this mask is most definitely ronin. It has nothing to do with the Samurai. It is singular, unique. Meant for defense, yes, but more so, meant to cover, to hide, one's face. A dishonored face."

Jaden pulled the mask over his head and pulled the buckles and straps tight. He faced the class.

The mask was black with reflective eyes. There was an awkward and lengthy pause. Someone laughed nervously.

"I am ronin," Jaden said twirling his katana once, then twice.

Although no one could see his eyes, his gaze settled on the back of the class. On a group of boys.

On Joshua.

Jaden stepped forward between the desks. He lifted his katana high.

First came the screams. Then the door to the classroom burst open and terrified students began streaming out in panic. Students ran every which way down the hallways, screaming at the top of their lungs. Soon other classroom doors opened and curious teachers and students stepped out into the hallways, wondering what the commotion was about. Their question was answered when the boy with the mask stepped out from the classroom and into the hallway.

Jaden walked down the hall slowly. His white tee-shirt was stained red, as were his pants and his mask. As was his katana. In his right hand he held his blade, dripping blood.

In his left hand he held Joshua's head.

He walked past open doorways and horrified faces, past shrieks and screams.

The door caught the sun and glinted as he stepped from the school and out into the swirling snow. He tossed the head away and walked farther down the walkway.

Finally, he stopped. He reached back, unbuckled the mask, and let it fall to the ground. He looked up into the sky as the snow touched his face.

He closed his eyes and cracked a slight smile. He dropped to his knees, and brought his katana out before him.

He paused for a moment, then stabbed himself in the stomach.
He did not scream or cry out. He was silent.
He fell forward. And soon the snow began to cover him.

978-0-595-47897-2
0-595-47897-2

Printed in the United States
112109LV00003B/352-360/P

9 780595 478972